A man on a train with a bullet in the center of his forehead . . .

A lady's cigarette case with an engraving of six bizarre-looking birds . . .

A dreamlike palace of nightmare terror ruled by a smiling and sinister oriental despot . . .

And two great nations on the brink of war . . .

All were but part of the maze of mystery and menace that Mr. Moto had to explore with excruciating care, as corpses littered the death-dark path, and murder waited around every blood-slick turn . . .

Also by John P. Marquand
and available from Popular Library:

YOUR TURN, MR. MOTO
THANK YOU, MR. MOTO
THINK FAST, MR. MOTO

MR. MOTO IS SO SORRY

by John P. Marquand

POPULAR LIBRARY • NEW YORK

Published by Popular Library, CBS Publications,
CBS Consumer Publishing, a Division of CBS Inc., by
arrangement with Little, Brown & Company (Inc.)

August, 1977

ISBN: 0-445-04033-5

CHAPTER 1

THE POLICE OFFICIAL in his shoddy gray suit of European clothes looked up from his notebook and papers with expressionless dark eyes and sucked in his breath politely. Calvin Gates had been in Japan less than a week, but it had been time enough to learn a good deal about the Japanese. They were watching, always watching, hundreds of impassive faces with their dark, bright eyes.

They were watching him now as he sat at a small table in the dining saloon of the boat which was to carry him across to Fusan in Korea. The dining room stewards were watching. Outside, near the gangway, a pair of squat muscular porters in cotton, kimonolike jumpers were watching. Two khaki-clad officers, each with heavy spectacles and a heavy saber, seated at a near-by table, were watching. He took off his hat and laid it on the table and passed his hand over his closely cropped, sandy hair. His hand seemed large and awkward, his whole body needlessly heavy. The damp, oily smell of dock-water came through an open window and with it sounds of efficient hoistings and bangings and of strange voices speaking a tongue-twisting language.

"Excuse," said the policeman. "You are an American?"

Calvin Gates agreed. His passport was on the table. He had been questioned so often that he no longer felt uneasy.

"You are thirty-two years old," the policeman said. "What does your father do?"

"He's dead," said Calvin Gates.

"Oh," the policeman said, "I am so sorry for you. You are a student? What do you study, please?"

"Anthropology," said Calvin Gates. It was an inaccuracy, but it could not make much difference.

"Oh yes," the police said. "What is anthropology?"

"The science of man," said Calvin Gates.

"Oh yes," the policeman repeated, "the science of man. You do not write books? You will not write books about Japan? You are just traveling through Japan?"

The American rested his lean freckled hands on the table and they seemed to him almost barbarously strong. The policeman studied his face, which was also lean and freckled, waiting for his reply. Calvin Gates blinked his grayish eyes and sighed. Suddenly he felt tired and homesick and entirely out of place.

"I have to travel through as fast as I can," he said.

"Oh," said the policeman. "How long have you been in Japan?"

"Less than a week," Gates answered. "Just long enough to make the necessary arrangements to go to Mongolia."

Was the man being dull, Gates wondered, or was he simply being officious? He was busy scribbling notes in his book and occasionally drawing in a sibilant breath.

"You pass on to Mukden?" the policeman said. "You do not stop?"

"Only for train connections," Gates answered.

"Oh yes," said the policeman, "oh excuse."

"From Mukden to Shan-hai-kuan," the traveler continued amiably. "From there I proceed to Peiping, and from there to Kalgan."

"Oh yes," the policeman said. "What do you do in Mongolia?"

"I have explained a good many times," Gates answered wearily. "I am joining a scientific expedition."

"Oh yes," the policeman said, "a scientific expedition. Where is the scientific expedition in Mongolia?"

"Inner Mongolia," Gates repeated patiently. "I am joining what is known as the 'Gilbreth Expedition.' The other members left here two weeks ago. I shall be told where I am to find them when I reach Kalgan. You must have seen them when they went through here."

"Oh yes," said the policeman. "Please why did you not go with them?"

6

"Because I could not make arrangements to come earlier."

"Thank you." The policeman wrote carefully in his book. "You go to find something in Mongolia? What do you go to find?"

"Primitive man," Gates said.

"Oh," said the policeman, "primitive man. You go and catch a man?"

The American blinked his grayish eyes.

"The man we're going to catch is dead," he said.

"Oh," said the policeman, "you go to catch a dead man?"

"Yes," said Gates, "the man we hope to catch has been dead at least a million years."

The policeman wrote carefully in his book.

"Oh," he said, "dead one million years. Here are your papers, please. So sorry for you we cannot talk longer. There are two other passengers."

The policeman rose and bowed, leaving Calvin Gates to wonder, not for the first time, what it was all about. Everything he said would be in his dossier. Doubtless someone in some office would check over all his ambiguous remarks. His desire to join the Gilbreth Expedition had been explained at meticulous length, but repetition did not seem to matter. Calvin Gates rose, picked up his trench coat and turned to walk out of the little dining saloon. He was moving toward the door when a voice said: "Oh, excuse me."

A small man had risen from a corner table and was smiling and bowing. He was carefully dressed in a neatly tailored blue serge suit. His linen was stiffly starched. His jet black hair was brushed stiff like a Prussian officer's.

"Excuse me," the little man said again. He was holding out a visiting card, a simple bit of oblong card on which was printed "I. A. MOTO." The name meant absolutely nothing, but Calvin Gates was not surprised.

"Are you the police too?" he asked.

"Oh no," the other said and laughed. "But I am friends of Americans. I have been to America. Shall we sit down and have some whisky? It would be so very nice."

Calvin Gates was beyond being astonished, for other

7

Japanese had been helpful before through no understandable motive.

"Thank you," he began. "It's getting late—"

"Oh no," said Mr. Moto, "please. Never too late for whisky in America. Ha! Ha! I admire America so much. I am so afraid that you are tired of our policemen."

Mr. Moto bowed and pulled back a chair and Calvin Gates sat down.

"So sorry," said Mr. Moto. "The policemen work so hard. Please, I have studied at college in America. I could not help but overhear. You are embarking on a scientific expedition for Mongolia? That will be very, very interesting and very, very nice. It is very lovely in Mongolia."

"Have you ever been there?" Calvin asked.

"Oh yes," Mr. Moto bobbed his head and smiled. "I have been to the region where you are going." Mr. Moto smiled again and clasped his delicate brown hands. "To Ghuru Nor."

Calvin Gates felt something jump inside him, and for the first time in many days he was uneasy. The little man was looking at him unblinkingly, still smiling.

"How do you know where I'm going?" he asked. "I never told the policeman that."

"Please'" said Mr. Moto. "Excuse me, please. I have read of it in the Tokyo newspaper. I am so interested. You see—in your country I studied anthropology. You are Nordic, Mr. Gates, with a trace of Alpine. Nordics are so very nice."

Calvin Gates took off his hat. Uneasiness, and a sudden feelings of being hunted and a suspect returned to him, although, after all, there was no reason why he should consider himself a fugitive.

"Please," said Mr. Moto. "I am so very interested. Geologically speaking the Central Asian plateau may have been the cradle for the human race so very nicely. Geologically the Himalayas are so new. Before they were thrust up, the animals and flowers of the land about the Malay Archipelago extended over Central Asia, did they not? The wooly rhinoceros was there and also the anthropoids. Then the Himalayas cut off those poor monkeys. Am I not right? To live, these creatures had to come down from

8

the trees. It is interesting to consider that they turned to men; very, very interesting. No doubt the ancestors of the Peiping Man are there. We have heard of bones in the deposits near Ghuru Nor. I am so very, very pleased that you are going, Mr. Gates."

"You certainly know all about it," Calvin Gates said. "Are you connected with some university?"

"Oh no," said Mr. Moto, "oh no, please." He smiled in the determined engaging manner of his race, displaying a row of uneven teeth, righly inlaid with gold. "There is only one thing which is—ha ha—so very funny."

Calvin Gates was unable to appreciate Mr. Moto's sociable merriment, nor could he tell whether its purpose was to put him at ease or not.

"Something's funny, is it?" he inquired.

"Yes," said Mr. Moto gleefully, "so funny. So sorry that I startle you perhaps."

"You don't startle me," said Calvin Gates.

There was an intense beady glint in the eyes of the small man opposite him, but his voice was smooth and genial.

"So glad I do not," said Mr. Moto. "Thank you. I have learned so many very lovely jokes in America. It is so funny that the primitive man, who lived so many years ago, should have selected such an interesting place to die. It is so funny that the drift where his bones rest at Ghuru Nor should be one the the most strategic points in the area between Russia and North China. So funny for the primitive man."

Mr. Moto laughed again and rubbed his delicate hands together. He was making such an obvious effort to be agreeable that Calvin's watchfulness relaxed.

"Are you an army officer?" Calvin asked him.

The beady look returned to Mr. Moto's eyes, and for a moment his smile was unnatural and fixed.

"No," he said, "not army—please. So nice to see Americans, and it is so very nice that you are going to Mongolia. Perhaps we can have a good talk tomorrow. I should like so very much to be of help. You may be lonely on the train tomorrow going through Korea, although there is your countrywoman going also on the train. She is on the boat now. Perhaps you know her?"

"A countrywoman?" Calvin Gates repeated.

"An American young lady," said Mr. Moto. "Yes. She is traveling with a Russian, who may be a courier I think. See, the policeman is talking to them now."

Calvin Gates glanced across the room. A slight dark girl in a brown tweed traveling suit was sitting with the policeman. He could tell she was an American without knowing why. He knew it even before she spoke in a drawling voice, and it occurred to him disinterestedly that she would have been good-looking if she had paid attention to her clothes. As it was, she did not appear interested in looks. It was as though she considered them as something best concealed.

"Yes," she was saying, "Winnetka, Illinois; born in 1910. It's on the passport, isn't it? And my color's white as a rule. And my father's a manufacturer."

"Oh," said the policeman, "yes, he makes things?"

"What did you think he did," the girl asked, "walk a tightrope?"

Her voice dropped to a monotone again and Mr. Moto sighed.

"It does no good to get angry," he said. "The poor policeman works so hard. You do not know the young lady?"

"No," Calvin Gates shook his head. "There's a large population in America. I've never met them all."

"A tourist, I suppose," said Mr. Moto. "You are going to Mongolia alone?"

It might have been imagination, but it seemed that Mr. Moto was watching him with unnecessary attention.

"As far as I know," said Calvin Gates.

"Oh," said Mr. Moto. "We will have a nice talk in the morning."

Calvin Gates rose and bowed. It seemed to him that he was always bowing and smiling until his facial muscles were strained from polite grimaces. The girl's voice, with its midwestern articulation, had been the only thing in two days that had reminded him of home.

When he passed along a narrow passage toward his

10

stateroom, a steward, a flat-faced, snub-nosed boy, bowed and hissed and opened his door and switched on the light. Calvin threw his hat and trench coat on the berth, seated himself on a small stool and took a notebook and pencil from his pocket.

"Second class to Shimonoseki," he wrote. "Mothers nursing babies. Old men taking off their clothes and scratching. Rice fields. Chatter, chatter. Rice wine. Soldiers. Clap clap of wooden shoes. Police. What does your grandfather do? Little boat. Mr. Moto, who knows anthropology. Fusan tomorrow, but must not take pictures."

He realized that his words would be unintelligible to most, but they would never be so to him. They would always bring back a hundred noises and faces and that sense of being an outlander in a train that ran through a country unbelievably like that country's pictures, with its tall blue hills, and bamboo, and tiny farms, with its concrete dams and its high tension wires and its factories, with its population half in kimonos and half in European clothes. It was a land of smiles and grimness, half toylike, half efficient.

He rose, took off his coat and glanced at his baggage. As soon as he did so he discovered that his brief case, which he had left beside his steamer trunk, had disappeared. He opened the door and shouted into the passageway.

"Boysan!" he shouted. The flat-faced room steward came running.

"Look here," Calvin Gates said, "where's the little bag, the one that was there?"

The flat brown face stared at him.

"Bag." Calvin Gates said to the boy. "Little bag, so big." The boy drew in his breath.

He spoke loudly, as one does when dealing with a foreigner, in the absurd hope that shouting might make the meaning clearer. Even while he spoke he knew that he was achieving nothing.

"Get someone who can speak English," Calvin Gates shouted. "All my notes—papers are in that bag."

At that same moment a door across the passageway opened, and Mr. Moto appeared, holding a small brown brief case in his hand, displaying his gold teeth and bowing.

"Oh," said Mr. Moto, "I am so very, very sorry. Can this be your bag? This ship boy was very stupid."

"Thanks," said Calvin Gates. "Thank you very much."

"Oh no," said Mr. Moto. "I am so glad to help. Good night until tomorrow."

"Good night," said Calvin Gates. He closed his door and sat down with his brief case across his knees. He was positive that he had seen the bag deposited in his own stateroom. He was positive that the bag had not been placed in Mr. Moto's room by mistake. Mr. Moto had been looking through his papers, but the papers were all there in the order he had left them—only a few personal letters, and nothing of any importance. He took out the last letter about Dr. Gilbreth, which had been written him by the Doctor's business representative in New York.

Dear Cal:—

You could have knocked me over with a feather when I got your letter asking how to find Gilbreth. He must have told you about the shooting in Mongolia. The office here will be in touch with him since we handle his accounts, but even a cable will take weeks sometimes to deliver. The best way to find him will be to go to the man in Kalgan who is seeing to his supplies and transportation. He is a part-German, part-Russian, who does trading in Mongolia by the name of Holtz. When you find him in Kalgan, he can probably get you out at a time when he is sending out supplies by motor.

Gilbreth has an artist going out to join him, a good-looking girl with a temper. You may meet her on the way, as she only left last week. Gilbreth was no end pleased by the check your uncle sent. It made all the difference in his being able to go, and it was like the old gentleman not to want any acknowledgment. Bella made that clear enough when she brought in the check. When you see him, be sure to thank him for us. . . .

There was nothing which was important, but it was obvious that Mr. Moto had been seeking something. Now that he thought of it, all of Mr. Moto's conversation had been more adroit than any of the questions of the police. He could almost believe that Mr. Moto's gentle words had been probing into his past, that there was something odd about him which Mr. Moto had seen but which no one else had noticed. He unfolded his map of China and Japan, and stared at it as he had twenty times before, still only half convinced that he was doing what he set out to do. He could locate himself at the narrow strait which separated Japan from the mainland of Asia, and he could see the curve of the railroad which started at the port of Fusan, and wound up through the promontory of Korea, and thence through Manchuria to Mukden. It would take twenty-four hours to reach Mukden by train provided there was no delay, and that would not be half the journey. He must pass the night at Mukden and take another train westward through Manchuria to Shan-hai-kuan by the Great Wall of China. There he must change and on the following morning he would arrive at Peiping, only to change trains again. Then he must travel north for another day's journey before he reached Kalgan. He had no way of telling how far he must travel after that—somewhere to the north where there was no railroad—until he could find Dr. Gilbreth to tell him what he wanted.

Long after he had folded the map again, when he tried to go to sleep he could see the line of railroads and those unknown cities.

CHAPTER 2

CALVIN GATES lay in his berth staring at the dark, while the steady beat of the engines, almost like the heart pulsations of a living organism, quivered rhythmically through the little ship. As he listened the whole vessel seemed alive, awake and conscious. There were knowing little creakings of the woodwork and strange premonitory shivers from the deck beneath. He knew that he would not sleep well that night, for it had been that way before, when his mind moved to vanished possibilities of what he might have said and what he might have done.

Finally he turned on the light and dressed. Then he put on his hat and coat and looked at his wrist watch. It was one o'clock in the morning and he new that the ship would be well out on that body of water which divided Japan from the mainland.

The key to his cabin door lay on the washstand and he picked it up, drew back the bolt, and turned the heavy brass doorknob. Outside, the narrow passageway which ran between the passengers' cabins was brightly lighted and empty. He closed his door and locked it, and tried the lock carefully before he put the key in his pocket. The dining-room doors were closed and the flat-faced room steward was sleeping in a folding chair. He walked by, careful not to wake him, up the stairs to the boat deck.

The ship was moving over a cool, placid sea. Her lights made little yellow pools on the gently undulating waves. As far as his sight carried there was no shore lights and no lights of other ships. He had the small deck entirely to himself, and the loneliness gave him a sense of comfort, and a feeling of motion without his own volition. It was pleasant to know that he was moving.

He was moving away from it, moving away. He was thinking that Central Park would be misty in the haze of a sultry summer day, when some half-heard sound brought his attention back to the rail where he was leaning and back to the quiet deck, with the rhythmical sounds of the engine and the whirr of the ventilator fans. He was sure that he never consciously heard a sound, yet he knew that he was not alone—he knew before he turned.

"Good evening," a voice said. "It is such a very lovely evening."

"Oh," Calvin said, "good evening." A man had moved beside him with soft, almost noiseless steps; it was his acquaintance of the early evening, the fragile Japanese gentleman, Mr. I. A. Moto.

"Ha ha," said Mr. Moto with a forced laugh. It seemed to Calvin that the Japanese were always trying to laugh.

14

"I find it hard to sleep on boats and trains. Ha ha, I am always wide awake."

"Yes," Calvin said politely, "I find it hard myself. I was thinking and I could not sleep."

"Oh," said Mr. Moto, "you were thinking?"

"Yes," said Calvin.

"Oh," said Mr. Moto, "you were thinking of New York?"

Mr. Moto's face was only a blur in the dark.

"How did you know I came from New York?" Calvin asked.

There was a sibilant hiss of politely indrawn breath from the blur of Mr. Moto's face.

"Excuse me, please," said Mr. Moto. "You have the New York voice. The young American lady on board comes from the Middle West. I like to think that I can always tell. New York is such a very lovely city. You like Tokyo? We are trying so hard to be like New York."

"I wonder why you do?" Calvin asked.

"Perhaps," said Mr. Moto, "we all admire your country so much, how it has reached out from such a little country and become so great."

"You're reaching out too, aren't you?" Calvin asked.

"Oh yes," said Mr. Moto. "We must live. We are such a little people."

"You've done a lot," said Calvin.

"It is so kind of you to say so," Mr. Moto said. "I hope so much you like Japan. We make so very many interesting things—so many small things which are so easy to carry. Our workmen are so very, very careful. Perhaps you have bought some small articles?"

The question was a part of that whole aimless conversation, which was so like his other conversations with other Japanese,—the exploits of Japan, the antiquity of Japanese culture, and Japan's peculiar mission in the Orient,—but something told Calvin that Mr. Moto was waiting, attentively waiting, for the answer to that trival question.

"Why yes," said Calvin. "I've bought some small things, nothing much."

"I am so glad," said Mr. Moto. "Perhaps you have

seen our silver work with the inlay of gunmetal cut right through the silver? It is so very nice. Perhaps you have bought a cigarette case of that work?"

"No," said Calvin, "I haven't."

"You do not smoke, perhaps," said Mr. Moto. "Those cases are so nice. There is an inlaid pattern of small birds flying through grasses. I am so very fond of it. Perhaps you have seen the pattern on silver? So very many little birds."

There was no doubt any longer that the talk was leading somewhere. Calvin understood that Mr. Moto was waiting patiently, not for an answer as much as for some change of voice. He knew he was not wrong when Mr. Moto spoke again.

"You have not seen the cases with the inlays of the little birds?"

"No," said Calvin.

"Ha ha," said Mr. Moto. "Excuse me, please. It is so very interesting that you are going to Mongolia. Ghuru Nor is very beautiful. Have you heard of the prince who lives there?"

"No," said Calvin. "Is there a prince?"

"Oh yes," said Mr. Moto brightly. "The men who are not priests wear pigtails. Such a very backward country. The prince's name is Wu Fang. That is his Chinese name, of course."

"Does he wear a pigtail too?" Calvin asked.

"Oh yes," said Mr. Moto. "He lives in a small palace and keeps camels. He has an army too. The Mongolians are very, very jolly."

"I'm glad to hear it," Calvin said.

"Oh yes," said Mr. Moto. "You will like it all so very, very much, that is if there is no trouble."

"Trouble?" Calvin repeated.

Mr. Moto laughed.

"Ha ha," said Mr. Moto. "I hope so very much that you will have no trouble."

"Well," said Calvin, "it's a complicated world. I think I'll go back and try to get some sleep."

"Yes," said Mr. Moto, "I shall go back too, I think. It

16

has been so very pleasant. Thank you very much. You first, please, Mr. Gates."

When Calvin walked down the stairs to the passageway with Mr. Moto just behind him, he felt the bewilderment he had experienced before when he had come in contact with an Oriental mind. He was sure that the conversation had not been aimless, although it led nowhere. Something in Mr. Moto's interest was disturbing. Even Mr. Moto's footsteps behind him were disturbing. He took his key from his pocket to open his stateroom door and the key did not turn in the lock.

"Excuse me," said Mr. Moto, "is there something wrong?"

"It's the key," Calvin told him; "it doesn't seem to work."

"So sorry," Mr. Moto said. "The key does not work? How very, very funny."

But it did not seem to Calvin that it was very funny.

"Look here," he said, turning on Mr. Moto, "what's all this about?"

"I do not know," said Mr. Moto. "We will go and find the boy."

The boy was still asleep in his chair near the dining saloon. Mr. Moto spoke sharply and the boy's eyes opened.

"The boy will know how," said Mr. Moto. "Let the boy try the key, please. Thank you very much."

The boy turned the key. The lock clicked and he opened the stateroom door.

"Ha ha," said Mr. Moto. "It is all right now, I think."

"Thank you," said Calvin. "It's all right now."

"So very glad," Mr. Moto said. "Good night."

Calvin Gates shot the bolt of his stateroom door again and looked grimly at his trunk and bags beneath the berth. When he had first tried the door someone had been inside; and now whoever it was had gone; and Mr. Moto was looking for a cigarette case with a design of little birds upon it, lots of little birds.

Whatever it was that Mr. Moto wanted, it was no affair of his, and he was able to go to sleep. He was able to dream of pigtails and of places of which he had no knowledge, and through his dreams he could hear Mr. Moto's voice.

"So very nice," Mr. Moto was saying, "so very, very nice."

CHAPTER 3

AT THE REAR of the train which left Fusan the next morning there was an observation car where Japanese businessmen and Japanese army officers sat and smoked and talked in sharp loud voices. The road for the most part followed river beds, back from which rose brownish hills and bluish mountains. There were green patches of farms near the river, but for the most part the country was bleak and rugged, and even the highest hills were bare of trees. That bareness gave the impression of a land which had been lived in for millenniums without much change. The Korean houses were like something from the stone age, round mud huts with curious mushroom-shaped thatch roofs. White-clad bearded men stood near them smoking pipes. White-robed farmers walked along the paths with their hands clasped behind them, wearing high black varnished hats perched airily above their heads.

It may have been because of the total unfamiliarity of the scene outside that Calvin experienced an increasing sensation of self-consciousness. He had not realized the extent of this malaise until he saw the girl whom he had seen on the boat the night before. She walked into the observation car, looked about her carelessly and selected one of the wicker chairs, lighted a cigarette and opened a book. Calvin Gates smiled and bowed, but she only nodded to him curtly as though to tell him that she did not need his company, and then he saw the reason. A shabbily dressed, youngish man entered the car a moment later and took the chair beside her.

The dress, the turn of the head, the smile, the familiarity with everything showed that he was not there for his own pleasure. The tilt of his head indicated his profession,

18

and the way his fountain pen was clipped into his upper coat pocket suggest its constant use in keeping a petty cash account. All those small details gave him that cosmopolitan quality common to all guides and couriers. He might have been a native of half a dozen countries from Norway to the Balkans, but he certainly was not an American. The cut of his clothes and the sharp point of his nose and chin and the motions of his hands indicated some other origin, and his voice also showed it even though it was devoid of any accent, the facile voice of a man of many tongues.

"Everything is safe in the baggage car, Miss Dillaway," Calvin heard him say. "They will look over the baggage again at Antung."

The girl turned her head with a sort of impatient annoyance, and slapped a firm brown hand down on her open book.

"For goodness' sakes, Boris," she said, "isn't this all Japanese territory?"

As soon as he heard the name, Calvin Gates understood the face and voice. The man was a Russian.

"It's only a formality, Miss Dillaway," he explained, looking at her with patient, slightly protruding, bluish eyes. "Antung is on the border of Manchukuo, a separate state you understand."

"Rubbish," said Miss Dillaway. "It's Japanese, isn't it?"

Then a curious thing happened. As Miss Dillaway was speaking, the blond Russian had glanced toward the door of the observation car, and at that same moment Mr. Moto appeared, a somewhat startling sight.

Mr. Moto was dressed in black-and-white checked sport clothes, and his spindly legs glowed in green and red golf stockings. For a moment Calvin Gates was tempted to laugh, but the inclination left him when he saw the face of Miss Dillaway's companion.

The bluish eyes of that blond young man had grown more protuding, and his hands had dropped slowly until they gripped the arms of his wicker chair.

"What's the matter with you, Boris?" Miss Dillaway was saying, "Are you sick?"

Her voice aroused the Russian from his reverie.

"Oh no," he said. "It is nothing, nothing."

"Well, don't look as though you'd seen a ghost," Miss Dillaway said. "You give me the creeps, and the Japanese are trouble enough."

"Please," Boris said hastily in low agitated tones. "They understand what you are saying."

"Well, let 'em understand," said Miss Dillaway. "I'm not doing any harm."

If Mr. Moto heard, he paid no attention. Without even bestowing a glance on them, he moved toward Calvin Gates.

"So nice to see you," Mr. Moto said, "so very nice."

"Good morning," Calvin answered. "Are you going to play golf, Mr. Moto?"

"Ha ha," said Mr. Moto. "I wear these clothes so often traveling, because they do not get out of press. I used to press so many trousers in America."

"Did you?" Calvin asked him.

"Oh yes," said Mr. Moto, "yes." He raised his hand before his mouth and drew in his breath. "When I was studying in America. They will examine the baggage at Antung and the policeman must see your papers. I should be so very glad to help you, if you would not mind."

"Thank you" said Calvin. "Hello, look at that!"

The train had stopped on a siding while they were speaking, and another train was going by them.

"Yes," said Mr. Moto, "soldiers. A troop train, I suppose."

A long train rolled by them with black heads of small khaki-clad men peering from its windows and then flat cars loaded with artillery, car after car of guns and caissons.

"It looks like a war," Calvin said.

"No, not a war," said Mr. Moto. "They are just soldiers, new soldiers. I am so very afraid that we will be delayed by troop trains. We will be very many hours late before we reach Mukden—so many hours."

Calvin looked out of the window with a new interest.

"Those guns look like German seventy-sevens," he said.

Mr. Moto's head had turned toward him with a birdlike sort of quickness.

"Not exactly," Mr. Moto said. "You understand artillery?"

"Yes," Calvin said, "a little."

He was aware that Mr. Moto was favoring him with his full attention.

"You are not," Mr. Moto said, "an army officer yourself?"

"No," Calvin answered, "but I've done quite a lot of military reading. Sometimes I've thought of being a soldier."

"Oh," said Mr. Moto. "You are so fortunate not to be a soldier. The breech mechanism of our field-pieces is different from light German guns. So sorry we will be delayed to let the troops go by."

There were soldiers enough in Korea, but when the train rolled the next day through what had been Manchuria iron hats and khaki uniforms and field equipment became part of the landscape, and the landscape itself had changed. The land had assumed a level, peaceful aspect, reminding him somewhat of a prairie state at home. There were small farms and narrow roads as far as he could see, and in some way, though the sight was new, it all appeared familiar. The country had begun to resemble the scenes on the blue-and-white china plates which had been placed before him as a child. There were the same houses with the same sweeping curves to their eaves, the same willow trees drooping above them, the identical bridges across the streams. The same figures, half reassuring and half grotesque, bent over fields or plodded with poles on their shoulders. The oddest sights seemed to fit into a sort of decorous order, impervious to change, and life rose robustly out of the earth in earthen houses and villages surrounded by high walls. Life sank back into the earth again, to a past which was marked by the mounds of ancestral graves that dotted corners of nearly every field.

The train was moving through this new country when he had his first conversation with Miss Dillaway. She appeared in the observation car about eight o'clock the next morning and took a chair next his and drew a timetable out of her pocketbook.

"Hello," Miss Dillaway said. "It's a funny country, isn't it? It looks like a plate."

"I'm sorry you thought of that," Calvin Gates said. "I had thought that was an original idea with me."

Miss Dillaway glanced out the window and wrinkled her nose.

"There's nothing original about any of it," she said. "It's been going on for two thousand years. Have you ever been out here before?"

"No," said Calvin, "never."

"Neither have I," said Miss Dillaway, "and I'd like to see a gas tank and a factory chimney."

"Didn't you see enough in Japan?" Calvin asked her.

"Japan!" Miss Dillaway laughed shortly. "It isn't permanent. It's almost pathetic to see those poor people trying." She nodded toward the fields and farms out the window. "All this is going to swallow them up in two or three hundred years. Maybe they realize it even now. They look like little boys playing soldier, don't they? And don't tell me not to say it out loud. I'm tired of being told to be quiet."

The train had stopped at a station as she spoke, similar to all the other wayside stations they had been passing. It was built of gray brick, evidently designed by some European engineer, and behind it was a cluster of brown mud houses which made two slovenly lines along a muddy street. All around the station building was a wall of white sandbags. A corporal's guard armed with rifles had filed from the station and stood at attention.

"Look at them," said Miss Dillaway. "They've gobbled up Manchuria and they still have to hide behind sandbags. It's pathetic, isn't it?"

"They don't look pathetic to me," Calvin said. "They look as if they knew their business."

"It's pathetic just the same," said Miss Dillaway, "because they won't get anywhere. Are you going as far as Peiping?"

Calvin Gates nodded. "Farther than that," he said, and Miss Dillaway seemed pleased.

22

"Then we'd better stick together," she said; "that is, if you don't mind. Frankly this county and this train are giving me the creeps, and that Russian guide I had, he's leaving."

"Leaving?" Calvin said.

Miss Dillaway wrinkled her nose again as though some smell in the car offended her.

"You've seen him, haven't you?" she answered. "The Russian with the fountain pen, who's been following me around? I'm no good with languages and I'm apt to lose my temper. I asked them at the hotel for a courier and they dug up Boris. I guess I don't understand foreigners very well. He's faded out on me. He gave me notice just after we came into this car yesterday morning. Something must have happened."

"What happened?" Calvin Gates asked.

Miss Dillaway made a careless gesture.

"You know how foreigners are," she said. "Boris was as nice as pie and suddenly he froze up and said he was leaving me at Mukden. I can't understand foreigners. It isn't my business. I just want to get where I'm going." She looked at him frankly. "I guess you don't care where you're going, do you?"

"What makes you think that?" Calvin asked.

"I'm sorry," said Miss Dillaway. "I've just been watching you on the train, the way you've been watching me, and you just gave me the idea that you didn't care where you were going. Do you mind telling me where you're going?"

Her question did not seem out of place, and he knew that her interest was friendly.

"Farther than Peiping," Calvin said. "I've been wanting to talk for two days to anyone except the police. I'm going to a place called Ghuru Nor. I'm looking for an expedition that's being run by a Dr. Gilbreth." He stopped because Miss Dillaway looked startled.

"What's the matter?" Calvin asked.

"Look here," said Miss Dillaway. "You don't look like anybody Gilbreth would take. You don't mean he's taking you?"

23

"Why shouldn't he?" Calvin asked. "At any rate I'm going to find him."

"No reason," Miss Dillaway said. "I'm interested because I'm going there myself."

Miss Dillaway looked at him again carefully and impersonally.

"What's your line, Mr. Gates?"

Her calm examination embarrassed him.

"I haven't got any line," he said. "What's your line?"

"Artist," said Miss Dillaway. "Painting scale pictures of pots and pans and skulls and landscapes. I've been on a lot of these things, but never into Asia. If you're going because of curiosity you won't like it. It's always hot and the food is always bad and everybody's always quarreling. It sounds all right when you get home, but it's terrible when you're there. I wouldn't do it if I weren't paid for it. Why are you doing it?"

Calvin Gates felt his face grow red. She would be the girl who was mentioned in the letter, the good-looking girl with a temper.

"For personal reasons," he said.

"Sorry," said Miss Dillaway. "I didn't mean to step on your toes, Gates. Well, as long as we've met, we'd better try to get there. It's nearly lunchtime, isn't it? Would you like to buy me a drink before lunch? They have some things in the dining car."

"Thanks," said Calvin.

Miss Dillaway walked ahead of him, briskly, her head and shoulders very straight. She sat down at one of the tables in the dining car and nodded to the chair opposite.

"Boy," she called, "whisky-soda. Is that what you want, Gates? Two whisky-sodas. Well, here's looking at you, Gates! Good luck!"

Calvin raised his glass. "If you don't mind my saying so," he said, "you don't seem very pleased that I'm going to Ghuru Nor. Of course, I didn't expect any loud applause." Calvin paused and smiled at her. "But I have some good points, you know. I might be useful."

Miss Dillaway set down her glass.

"Forget it, Gates," she said. "This is business for me, and you're one of these people looking for adventure.

24

You haven't been on as many of these things as I have. I've been in Persia and I've been bitten by fleas in the Mesopotamian Desert, and I've been in Central America, and the west coast of Africa. I go because I earn my pay, and I've seen lads who go for fun. They generally make trouble. They sit around the camp and just make trouble. There's nothing else for 'em to do. I don't mean it personally."

"I can carry your sketchbooks," Calvin said.

"Don't be silly," said Miss Dillaway. "As long as we're going, we've got to get acquainted. You're probably a nice boy. I hope you are."

"Thanks," said Calvin.

"Don't get touchy," said Miss Dillaway. "I never fight with anybody on expeditions." She raised her hand in front of her mouth and drew in her breath. "Who is that Japanese friend of yours? The one with the gold teeth and the golf stockings?"

"His name is Moto," said Calvin. "He picked me up on the boat."

"Well, he's tried to pick me up all day," Miss Dillaway said. "That's why I picked you up instead, Gates. Look, here comes Boris. He always hangs around when he thinks I'm going to take a drink."

She was right. The blond Russian was walking down the aisle, hesitating, smiling.

"Sit down, Boris," said Miss Dillaway. "This is Mr. Gates. What are you going to have, vodka?"

Boris clicked his heels together and shook hands.

"I am so happy to make your acquaintance, sir," he said. "Anything, my dear Miss Dillaway, anything at all."

"No use being polite," Miss Dillaway replied. "You guaranteed to see me through, and now you're walking out on me."

Boris sat down. There was a look of pained concern in his protuberant, bluish eyes.

"But I have explained," he said. "There was a message from my wife. I have told you and I have told you—she is ill and I must go back. Nothing short of the most serious news—"

25

"Forget it," said Miss Dillaway. "There's your vodka, Boris."

"Your very good health," Boris said. "Now that you have found a fellow countryman everything will be easy. The hotel porter will see you on the train at Mukden, and there will be a man to care for the baggage at the Shan-hai-kuan customs. I have really been superfluous, my dear Miss Dillaway. You manage all without me."

"All right," said Miss Dillaway. "You see me into the hotel at Mukden and you'll get your pay. We've been all over it, Boris."

But Boris was still deeply worried. His manner was ingratiating and contrite. His voice was placating and anxious.

"Just once again, Miss Dillaway," he said, "I am so sorry. I can take no pay from you for what I have done. Instead, if you please. I should like to make a peace offering." He put his hand in his inside pocket and cleared his throat. "I should like to give this to you as a peace offering. It is a silver cigarette case. Perhaps you saw them in Japan, with the dark metal inlay that goes all the way through it. Will you please accept it, Miss Dillaway?"

His speech was elaborate and formal, and Calvin Gates was also cynical enough to believe that the gesture was not made for nothing. The Russian had produced a small silver cigarette case such as a lady might carry in her bag, certainly of no great intrinsic value. He laid it almost timidly on the table in front of Miss Dillaway, where it rattled with the glasses in time to the vibration of the train. It was only when she picked it up that something flashed in Calvin Gates's memory. The cover was deco-rated by a design of reeds and birds, a number of little birds flying among grasses. As she held it, Mr. Moto's voice came through his memory, gentle, softly modulated.

"Very beautiful," Mr. Moto had said, "little birds, lots of little birds."

The Russian's forehead was moist and he spoke again with genuine feeling.

"It is not worthy of you," he said; "but I beg you to accept it, Miss Dillaway, and use it if you can, and I will take no pay."

Miss Dillaway picked up the case carelessly.

"Thanks," she said. "That's kind of you, Boris. You'll get your pay at Mukden. There's no use going through gestures about it."

"Please, my dear Miss Dillaway," the courier said. "I'm afraid you mistake the purpose of my little gift."

"Never mind," said Miss Dillaway, "thanks. Now run along, Boris. I want to talk to Mr. Gates. I'll see you in the hotel tonight at Mukden."

Boris rose and clicked his heels together and Miss Dillaway sighed.

"Putting me under obligations, isn't he?" she said. "I have a cigarette case already. It's a simple little game, isn't it?" And she opened her bag and dropped the cigarette case inside it. "Do you want one of my cigarettes? It's the same sort of case you see with a different design. What's the matter, Gates?"

"Nothing," said Calvin. "It's a pretty cigarette case."

"That isn't what you were thinking," Miss Dillaway said.

That was all that happened, an obscure incident in a long and tedious journey. There was nothing, when he thought of it later, that was peculiar, except that sight of little birds inlaid in black upon the silver.

When the train pulled into the shed at Mukden,—hours late, as Mr. Moto had predicted,—it had only been a tedious journey that had ended in a disorderly rush of porters. They arrived in the early evening and Calvin saw Boris through the coal smoke helping with Miss Dillaway's bags, and then, when Gates was moving away from the train indecisively, Mr. Moto stepped beside him.

"I should be so pleased to take you to the hotel," said Mr. Moto. "It is so confusing here at night."

"Thanks," said Calvin, "thank you very much."

"It is such a pleasure," said Mr. Moto. "It must be interesting here to a stranger."

Mr. Moto was right; even in the dark it was interesting. The air had a cold, nervous quality, and a thousand different sounds carried through it in the dark. It was a new, dark world, full of twinkling lights and voices, and it made him forget about the boat and train, as a traveler forgets such incidents almost as soon as they are over.

CHAPTER 4

IN FRONT of the station in the dark, while Mr. Moto signaled for a taxicab, it seemed to him that the place was full of violent memories of war and the rumors of war. He did not need daylight to know that he was at a crossroads, where tides of empire had met and ripped and swirled. The square outside the station, and the droshkies which were waiting beside the automobiles and rickshaws, showed that Russia had been there once. A beggar woman in blue rags came cringing up to them, holding out her hand. Mr. Moto spoke to her sternly and she went away.

"Not Chinese," Mr. Moto explained. "A Russian woman in Chinese clothes. Mukden is so nice. There are so very many points of interest. I hope so much that you can see them."

"I'm going on tomorrow," Calvin said.

"Oh," said Mr. Moto, "so sorry for you that you cannot see them. Here is the motor, please."

The sound of motor horns broke in on his voice, while he talked precisely about the unfortunate incident which had precipitated the crisis ending in the establishment of the Manchukuo state.

"You must understand," said Mr. Moto, "that the Chinese make everything so very difficult."

"Is that why you have soldiers at all the stations?" Calvin asked.

"Ha ha," said Mr. Moto, "yes, the soldiers at all the stations."

The hotel, like the droshkies, must have dated back to the Russian days. Once he was inside, except for the Japanese attendants, he might have been in a provincial

French hotel. There was the same slow-moving lift, the same broad staircases and ornate woodwork.

Miss Dillaway was already at the desk. She waited for him while he was assigned a room.

"Well, I've paid Boris off," she said. "Will you have dinner with me? How about meeting down here in half an hour?"

Calvin glanced at Mr. Moto.

"Please," said Mr. Moto hastily, "I have so much to do tonight. The manager is a friend of mine." He waved at a gray-haired Japanese gentleman in a morning coat, who stood behind the desk. "I shall dine with the manager."

She was waiting for him half an hour later, her hair pulled tight back from her forehead, her face shining and guiltless of powder.

"Well," said Miss Dillaway. "I hope your room's better than mine. I always thought the Japanese were clean, but I don't think my room's clean. I wonder where Boris went."

"Isn't he here?" Calvin asked.

Miss Dillaway shook her head. She was still in her brown tweed suit and she made a small lonely uncompromising figure in the high-ceilinged, dingy dining room, like a girl in a boarding school, he thought.

"The food's bad, isn't it?" she said. "I wouldn't touch that salad if I were you, Gates. I don't know why that Russian still bothers me. I don't know whether I hurt his feelings, or what. Foreigners are touchy, aren't they? Look at your Japanese friend looking at us."

"Don't worry about the Russian," Calvin said.

"I only worry about him," Miss Dillaway answered, "because he always looked so worried. He was like the White Rabbit in *Alice in Wonderland,* always startled like a rabbit. The only thing I don't worry about is myself, I guess. I suppose I'll start bothering about you next."

"Why?" asked Calvin.

Miss Dillaway's eyes grew narrow, and she smiled at him.

"I don't know," she said. "Maybe it's this air. You act as though something was the matter with you."

"Perhaps you frighten me," Calvin said.

29

"Don't be silly, Gates," said Miss Dillaway. "I don't frighten you and you know it. The trouble is you don't get anywhere with me. That's it, isn't it? You've never seen anyone who could look out for herself probably. Well, I can, and that's why I'm going to get some rest. Good night, Gates."

Calvin rose and bowed.

"And don't get into trouble, Gates," Miss Dillaway said. "I want to see you on the train tomorrow. Where's my bag?"

Calvin handed it to her.

"I must be losing my wits," she said. "It's the first time I've let that bag out of my hand. Take care of yourself. Good night."

"I'm going up too," Calvin said. "I'll see you as far as your room."

Calvin opened the tall French window of his hotel room and stepped out on a small balcony in front of it and drew a deep breath of the night air. Down below him he could see the lights of automobiles and carriages, and he could hear the sounds of horns and the clatter of hoofs. Behind him his room was almost comfortable— a single wooden bed with his baggage piled in front of it, a green carpet, a bureau and a writing table, and cream-colored, painted walls, and a single electric light that hung suspended from the center of the room. Life had become a succession of similar rooms, varying in comfort and discomfort.

He stood at the window, thinking of Miss Dillaway, and his thoughts were puzzled and confused, for he could not tell whether he liked her or not; he had never seen anyone like her. She was as lonely as he was and as out of place in those surroundings. It would surely not have been difficult for her to have been friendly, and yet it seemed to him that each time she had started to be friendly she had stopped herself deliberately. She had been like someone who was playing a part, like someone trying to be something she was not. More than once she had actually tried to be unattractive, and her casual rudeness had a note which did not ring true. He was almost sure of that, for now and then when she was not thinking she had lost all mannerism. He had seen it happen once across the table that evening. Her lips had lost their habitual defiant twist and her face instead of looking harsh and sharp had grown delicate and sensitive. He had been surprised once by its beauty, a dark, patrician sort of beauty, and even her voice had changed; it was as though she had forgotten herself, because a moment later her face was sharp again. He had tried to reassure her; he had tried to make her see that there was no reason to be afraid of him.

"And she never lets her purse go," Calvin said to himself. "She's just the kind that wouldn't."

His wrist watch had a luminous dial. He looked at it when he awoke that night. It was twenty minutes before twelve and someone was tapping on his door, softly but insistently. The light switch was just above the table by his bed. When he pulled it, the light glowed dimly. A breeze swayed the curtains before his open window, and the sound outside his door continued, a furtive, gentle knocking. He got into his slippers and put on his trench coat.

"What's the matter out there?" he began, and then his eyes became accustomed to the dimly lighted hall, Miss Dillaway's former courier, the Russian named Boris, stood outside the door.

"Hello," Calvin said to him. "What do you want?"

He found himself growing indignant as he spoke. It was exactly as Miss Dillaway had said: the man was like the White Rabbit in *Alice in Wonderland*. He was smiling placatingly; his forehead was moist with perspiration.

"I beg your pardon, sir," he said. "I wonder if I might come in."

"What's the matter with you?" began Calvin. He might have gone further, but something in the other's expression stopped him more than any explanation could have. The man in front of him was fighting against some sort of fear, and he was controlling that fear with a visible effort.

"I beg your pardon, sir," he said again. "I appreciate

31

you irritation, quite. I shall only be a minute. It is just one matter that is important."

Calvin Gates felt a strange, tingling sensation at the base of his spine. It did not require any explanation for him to realize that there was something wrong. Some ugly, unseen thing was coming to him out of the dullness of that journey. Some implication was being conveyed by that stranger's anguish.

"Come inside," Calvin said. "What's the matter with you, Boris?"

Boris came inside and closed the door behind him.

"Thank you, sir," he said. "I shall only be a moment. I do not think there is any danger."

"Danger," said Calvin, "what danger?"

The Russian blinked his blue eyes and smiled.

"It is just a manner of speaking, sir," he said. "I—have been distressed by something—a little detail about Miss Dillaway."

"What about Miss Dillaway?" Calvin asked him. "What's the matter?"

"Nothing," said Boris, "nothing really. It is only a simple detail—but I fear I have not been gentlemanly. I gave her a cigarette case. If you are traveling with her, sir, it might be better if you took it. A friend of mine may ask for it. I promised it to him—and if you will give it—" His voice was very low, almost expressionless.

"Who?" Calvin said. "What are you talking about?"

Boris moistened his lips before he answered, and he seemed to find the answer difficult.

"That is all, sir," he said. "It was intended for a friend of mine. I did not think at the time." His voice trailed off almost into a whisper, and Calvin stared at him grimly.

"You're going to do some thinking now," he said. "You've run into the wrong person this time. You're going to tell me what this is about before you get out of here."

Boris moistened his lips again and shrugged his shoulders.

"It is nothing," he began. "I was foolish to speak of it, perhaps. But a friend of mine will ask for it. Miss Dil-

32

laway might not understand. She is so—determined. I do not want her to be hurt. You see—a friend of mine—"

He paused, seemingly searching for a word, and his mouth had fallen open. He was staring beyond Calvin Gates in the direction of the French window, just as a creaking sound and a fresh gust of air made Calvin turn in the direction of Boris's startled glance.

The window had been pushed open quickly, and a small and stocky man stepped from the balcony halfway into the room. When he thought of it afterward, Calvin Gates had only an indefinite impression of him—of a broad, flat-nosed face, tightly closed lips and steady dark eyes, and dark somber European clothes. It was not the face but the action that Calvin Gates recalled, and the action was completely smooth and steady, giving no impression of haste. The man was holding a pistol, leveling it with the almost gentle motion of an expert marksman. In that fraction of a second, while Calvin gazed unbelievingly, he could see that the weapon was equipped with a silencing device—he could even recognize the model. Then, before anyone moved or spoke, there was a single shot, which came with a sound not much louder than that of an airrifle. There was no word, nothing but the breeze from the open window and that sudden sound. The eyes of Boris grew wide and staring; his knees buckled beneath him. Calvin reached toward him instinctively, but Boris was a dead weight, sinking to the floor. He was sinking to the floor with a bullet hole drilled through the center of his forehead, just above his eyes, a perfect shot both merciful and merciless. He had died without a word. When Calvin Gates looked up the window and the balcony were empty. It had all been as perfect and as inevitable and as accurately rehearsed as a moment in the theater. It had been cold-blooded murder done by an expert in the art, and so completely done that there was nothing left but silence.

Calvin Gates had never seen a dead man, but no experience was necessary to make the signs familiar. The mark on the forehead with the few drops of blood that oozed from it made him stand paralyzed, incapable of consecutive thought.

The night breeze still waved the dingy window curtains and the room was so quiet that he could hear the curtains scrape against the panes and sashes. That gentle and insignificant noise reminded him that everything had been discreet. Whoever it was who had fired the shot must have been standing on the balcony listening by the window, and he must have moved from some other room which opened on that balcony. Whoever it was had desired secrecy and silence. Calvin Gates drew a deep breath and the color came back to his freckled face.

His thoughts went no further because of a sound outside the door of his room. There was a click and the knob was turning. At the same instant he realized that the door was no longer locked.

There was no time to make a move, if he had wished to make one, before Mr. Moto had opened the door and closed it softly behind him.

"Oh," Mr. Moto said very gently. "He is—liquidated?"

CHAPTER 5

CALVIN STARED BACK without answering and there seemed to be no adequate answer. Mr. Moto had changed from his sport suit into a modest suit of black. He stood beside the closed door examining the dead man without a trace of surprise. Not a line of his delicate features moved, but his eyes were lively and very bright. Finally Mr. Moto drew in his breath with a soft, sibilant hiss.

"So sorry for you," Mr. Moto said, "so very, very sorry. You did not kill him I think." Calvin had intended to be impersonal and calm, but Mr. Moto's question broke down his resolution.

"No," Calvin said, "I guess you know I didn't."

"Please," Mr. Moto's voice was hardly more than a whisper. "Do not speak so loudly. I am so sorry for you, Mr. Gates. I could not help but hear the sound."

"What did you hear?" Calvin asked him. "You were

34

listening, were you? Why? What are you sneaking around me for?"

Mr Moto raised a fragile, coffee-colored hand.

"Please," he said. "It will be nice if you will please be reasonable. You were here in this room alone with this man who is now dead. I saw him enter, Mr. Gates."

"And what business was it of your if he did?" Calvin said.

"Please," said Mr. Moto again. "It would be so very nice if you were calmer, Mr. Gates. Do not concern yourself with who I am, please. I must ask you to sit in that chair by the writing table, please."

Before he spoke, Calvin took a careful step toward him.

"You go to the devil," he said, "unless you're going to try to kill me first."

"No," said Mr. Moto, "no please. It would not help. It would be so very nice if you would sit down—in the chair by the writing table, please. Do you not think it would be very, very nice?"

Mr. Moto smiled as he asked the question. There was a moment's silence and Calvin drew his trench coat around him and scowled.

"All right," he said. "I'm sitting down."

"So sorry for you," Mr. Moto said. "If you will excuse me, please."

Mr. Moto was displaying the sprightly impersonality of an undertaker, and it was apparent that he had dealt with similar situations. All his movements were adroit and unhurried like those of a hunter who finally moves to the point where the game has fallen.

"So too bad," Mr. Moto said, "so very, very clumsy."

First he knelt beside the body and touched it delicately. Then his hands moved flutteringly through the dead man's pockets, but it was evident to Calvin that Mr. Moto did not find what he wanted.

"So too bad," he murmured again, "so very, very clumsy."

Finally he rose from his knees, dusted his trousers carefully, clasped his hands together and bowed.

"And now I must ask a favor," Mr. Moto said. "It

35

would be so much nicer for me and for you if you will grant this favor. Do not be angry, please."

Calvin Gates understood at once that Mr. Moto was not asking a favor—he was making a definite request.

"What do you want?" Calvin repeated.

The answer was hesitant, but the hesitation was only make-believe; every intonation and every gesture of Mr. Moto's was coldly precise.

"So sorry," Mr. Moto said. "It is all such a very bad mistake. We are so happy to die for our Emperor—sometimes we do too much."

"What do you want?" Calvin repeated.

"That you will allow me to search your person," Mr. Moto said. "I shall do so with the greatest respect. It is simply a matter of passing my hands over the pockets of your coat and over your pajamas. Such a simple matter."

"Suppose I don't agree?" Calvin asked.

"Then," Mr. Moto said, "someone else would do it."

"You've been through all my baggage," Calvin said. "Isn't that enough?"

"I am so sorry," Mr. Moto said. "Nothing was taken. Will you please stand up?"

Calvin stood up and Mr. Moto's hands touched him gently.

"So kind of you," said Mr. Moto, "so very, very kind. I suppose you are thinking of so many things. You are wondering what we are going to do. If you will help, everything will be so nice."

"It would be a whole lot easier," Calvin said, "if you didn't talk about things being nice. There doesn't seem to be much for me to do, does there? A man comes in here, a stranger, and he's killed in front of me."

Mr. Moto lighted a cigarette and perched himself carefully on the edge of the bed.

"It was all so very clumsy," Mr. Moto said. "He should not have been killed. It was all such a very bad mistake." Mr. Moto smiled brightly. "The best we can do is to forget. Do you not think it would be nicer, Mr. Gates?"

"Forget?" repeated Calvin.

Mr. Moto nodded and smiled.

"It has all been so bad," he repeated. "So much better

36

to say nothing about mistakes. Will you listen to me for a moment, please?"

Calvin did not answer and Mr. Moto continued as though he had hit upon a happy social stratagem.

"You must not mind so much about so little. You are on a journey, and I hope so much that you will have a very happy journey."

Mr. Moto paused. The words were charmingly soft, but Calvin could feel an insistence behind them which resembled a threat.

"Go ahead, Mr. Moto, I am not a fool," he answered.

"Oh no. You are not a fool, Mr. Gates," Mr. Moto agreed cordially. "Because you are not a fool, I make a suggestion, a humble, nice suggestion."

"Go ahead," said Calvin.

"If you agree," said Mr. Moto, "I shall speak to my friend, the manager. He is so very nice to tourists. He will give you another room and your baggage will be brought there. This will only be a little secret, and I hope so much that you will say nothing, particularly to that young lady, Miss Dillaway. She would be very much disturbed. I hope so much that you understand me. If you do not you will not have a happy journey."

"Is that a threat?" asked Calvin.

"Please," said Mr. Moto. "That is not a nice word. I am trying so very hard. It is not a threat, but a request, I am so afraid. I am so sorry for you. You are suspected by the police."

Calvin felt his face change color, while Mr. Moto sat there watching him.

"You better tell me what you mean," he said.

"Oh yes," said Mr. Moto, "I shall be so very glad. You are going to such a strange place, Mongolia. My country is so interested in Mongolia. You say you are a scientist. That is not so, Mr. Gates. Do not interrupt me, please. We have means of information. You did very badly at Yale University. You have been in businesses since, but not successful. You have won some prizes at shooting with the rifle and the revolver. It is so funny you should be traveling, please—There are so many funny people in

Asia, Mr. Gates. So many are here to get away from their police."

Mr. Moto leaned forward slightly and his glance was fixed steadily on the other's face.

"I'm afraid you are a dangerous man, Mr. Gates, although I cannot be quite sure. I think perhaps that you might like to kill me. Do not try it, if you please."

Calvin Gates put his hands in the pockets of his trench coat.

"I might try if I had the chance," he said. "I don't like you, Mr. Moto."

"So sorry," Mr. Moto answered. "But you will listen please. I received a telegram about you tonight. The police in your country are looking for you, Mr. Gates."

Calvin Gates hesitated before he answered. He tried to keep his face composed and to hide whatever it was he felt, and he could understand at last the reason for all of Mr. Moto's interest. He was in something that was very close to danger.

"The police?" he said. "You must be crazy."

"No," said Mr. Moto. "So sorry to be rude. There are so many people in Asia wanted by the police. It will be so much nicer in Mongolia. There are no police in Mongolia."

Calvin passed his hand across his forehead.

"That can't be so," he said. "There must be something wrong somewhere. They wouldn't do that. He wouldn't. It was a family matter, Mr. Moto. I can explain it to you, if you want. There must be some mistake."

But Mr. Moto's face showed him that there was no mistake.

"Please," Mr. Moto said, "there is no reason to explain. You can help me, so very much. If you will travel quickly, everything will be so nice."

"What do they want me for?" Calvin asked.

Mr. Moto smiled and drew in his breath.

"For taking money," he said. "Excuse my rudeness, please. Someone has been taking a great deal of money from a gentleman in New York for several years. He says that it is you. I hope so much they are not right."

"For several years?" Calvin repeated, and his face felt

moist and clammy. "It was only once—it wasn't for several years. It was my uncle—it was a family matter. He wouldn't—he couldn't have called in the police. He's too much of a man for that—"

Mr. Moto drew in his breath again.

"So sorry," he said. "But you do not want to go back. I think. Please, am I not right?"

For a moment Calvin's mind moved back sickeningly into the past.

"I never knew that she'd done it before," he said, and his freckled face looked ugly. "But it's like her, though, and it's like her to get out from under—that girl would lie her head off—"

He stopped, suddenly realizing that Mr. Moto was no friend of his.

"You're right," he said, "I don't want to go back. If I could, I wouldn't want to. It would kill him if he knew about it. I'm going ahead to see this through. I've got to get there to see this Gilbreth."

Mr. Moto rose from his seat on the bed and stood before Calvin. His manner had changed to a sort of businesslike precision, which took Calvin off his guard. He realized that in his agitation at the news he had said a good deal more than he intended.

"It is so much nicer," Mr. Moto said, "now that we understand each other. I think we will get along so very nicely, if you are careful, Mr. Gates."

Mr. Moto pointed a delicate finger at him and nodded solemnly.

"Believe me, you must be careful, please. I am so used to bad men, Mr. Gates. They do not frighten me, not very much. I should not enjoy it if you had your hands upon my throat. I was so very happy that you have no weapons in your baggage. You look so gentle, but I think that you are dangerous, and able to think."

Calvin Gates scowled at Mr. Moto, "So nice of you to say so," he answered, "but you're wrong. I'm a sentimental fool, or I wouldn't be here tonight."

Mr. Moto raised his hand in polite agreement.

"Oh yes," he said, "Nordics are never very logical. I am not asking what you have done, Mr. Gates. You are

39

wanted by the police for taking money, but you are more than a thief I think. I do not ask about you, and you do not ask about me."

Calvin Gates's forehead was smoother.

"I don't ask about you," Calvin said, "because I don't give one continental damn."

"Thank you," said Mr. Moto, "so very much. I am glad that you say it clearly. Our authorities have been asked to detain you, but I think it can be arranged perhaps. So nice that I have influence."

"Detain me?" repeated Calvin Gates.

"Yes," said Mr. Moto, "yes."

"All right, you want me to keep still," Calvin told him. "Anything else, Mr. Moto? I'm ready to oblige, as long as I can keep on going."

Mr. Moto rubbed his hands together very softly.

"You will leave tomorrow on your journey as if nothing had happened," he said. "There is only one thing more. There is a cigarette case inlaid with little birds. It is not here."

Calvin Gates answered almost cordially.

"If that's what you want," he said, "I can get it for you. It might have been easier if you'd just asked for it before."

Mr. Moto shook his head very quickly.

"It is exactly what I do not want, please," he said. "I know where the little case is now, since you do not have it. You will do nothing and forget about it altogether. This is very important, please."

"All right," said Calvin Gates. "I don't know what your game is, but I'll forget it."

"I am so very glad," Mr. Moto said, "that you should understand. It is a very important game, please. I should not hesitate to go very, very far in it. I do not want anything disturbed. And now I shall show you to your room. It will be right across the hall, and I hope you will have a very pleasant night and such a very pleasant journey."

Calvin Gates stepped carefully past the dead man near the door.

"Well," he said, "I suppose I'll be seeing you again."

"I hope not," said Mr. Moto gently. "For your sake, Mr. Gates."

Calvin Gates hesitated. He knew so little that he could not tell how far to go; he only knew that he had been caught up in something entirely beyond his own control, and that he was not the only one who was caught. He was thinking of Miss Dillaway with her hair tied in an uncompromising knot, who made no effort to appear attractive.

"So you know who has that case?" he asked.

"Yes," said Mr. Moto, "I am so sure that I know now." He nodded toward the dead man. "Since he does not have it, and you have not. It was very important that the case should go where you are going. I wish so much for it to go there without trouble. It must. This was all such a bad mistake."

"It seems to me," said Calvin, "that it will be dangerous for Miss Dillaway."

Mr. Moto's expression gave no hint of agreement or disagreement.

"It will be dangerous for you if you should meddle," Mr. Moto said.

"Thanks," Calvin Gates answered, and he paused, and he and Mr. Moto looked at each other carefully. "I won't forget that, Moto."

"I am so glad," Mr. Moto breathed softly, "so glad you won't forget. I should be so sorry for you. May I show you your new room, please? It is right across the hall. I am so sorry, I shall be busy here tonight, so that we cannot have a pleasant talk."

The room where Mr. Moto took him was almost the same as the one he had left.

"Your bags will arrive in a few minutes," Mr. Moto said. "I am sorry I must leave you, I am so very busy."

CHAPTER 6

WHEN MR. MOTO LEFT him, Calvin opened the window and peered out into a dark courtyard; then he closed the window and stood with his ear close to the door listening

41

to sounds from the room across the hall. He could hear a soft thud of footsteps, and he could hear Mr. Moto's voice speaking in an insistent undertone.

He had not been listening long before there was a knock at his door. Two men who were obviously not hotel attendants carried his trunk into the room. They gazed at him incuriously and set the trunk at the head of the bed, and returned a moment later with his brief case and his bag. One of them brought in his clothes, which he laid carefully on a chair. Calvin took a piece of money from his trousers pocket, but they looked at him blankly and shook their heads. He heard them hurry across the hall again, open a door and close it, and a moment later he opened his own door. The hallway stretched before him to right and left, absolutely empty, and Calvin closed his door noiselessly and smiled. He had been surprised at first that his room had not been watched, but now he was not surprised: the thing that he proposed to do was so obvious that only a fool would have attempted it, and Mr. Moto had said that he was not a fool.

He turned out the light and dressed quickly in the dark. Then he opened the door again and stepped out into the hall, holding his shoes in his hand. He dropped them noisily in front of his door and listened. There was a confused and gentle murmur of voices in the room across the hall. Standing in the hallway, Calvin Gates slammed his door shut, and ran on tiptoe down the hall. He had judged the distance he must travel and the chances he must take.

He darted along the corridor in his stocking feet past the well of the lift to the stairway. When he reached the angle of the stairs, he paused in its shelter and looked behind him. He had moved quickly and just quickly enough. Not a second after he had reached the stairs the door of the room he had first occupied opened and Mr. Moto's head appeared. Mr. Moto was looking across the hall toward the shoes. Calvin Gates could not help smiling at their guilelessness. Mr. Moto gazed at them before he closed the door again, and Calvin's smile grew broader.

"I guess," he murmured, "Mr. Moto has put me in bed for the night."

42

He waited for a few moments, but the hall was empty. Finally he stepped from the angle of the stairs and continued moving softly down the corridor. He had seen Miss Dillaway to her room that night, and he remembered the number. He knocked upon her door without any hesitation, because the noise was a chance that he was obliged to take and he had realized long ago that when one started it was always better to move ahead. He knocked three times, and when he paused he was relieved to hear the key in the lock. A moment later Miss Dillaway opened the door a crack. He could not see her, but he heard her voice—a voice that was soft and incredulous.

"What's the matter, Gates?" she asked. "What is it?"

Calvin pushed the door open and he was in her room before he answered.

"Don't make a noise," he whispered.

He had forgotten about propriety and she had only been an abstraction to him until he was in her room, but when he was there he felt a self-conscious embarrassment at his rudeness. He had broken in upon something which he was not meant to see, upon a different person from the girl he had known on the train and upon a sort of privacy that made him stare at her blankly. She had on a negligee of delicate pastel green. Her bare feet were thrust into green silk mules, and her hair fell over her back and shoulders in a dark, misty cloud that framed the delicate oval of her face. Even with the startled look in her wide brown eyes her face was beautiful. In that moment of surprise she was very young and entirely untouched by the world outside.

The bare ugliness of the room had been changed by her small possessions—a gold-backed comb and brush upon the bureau, and some books on a chair. Her small blue leather traveling clock was on the table. They were all small things, but all of them made her different and all of them told him that he should not be there. For a second she was breathless and confused, and he shared her confusion.

"What do you mean by coming in here?" she said breathlessly. "What do you mean by pushing the door open?"

"I'm sorry," said Calvin Gates. Her face was growing red and so was his. "I didn't mean to startle you. I haven't got much time."

Miss Dillaway bit her lower lip and pulled her green gown more tightly about her, a quick instinctive gesture which reminded him that he was staring at her.

"Gates," she said, "are you going to get out of here or shall I have to ring? I didn't think you'd act like this. You're like all the rest of them. I thought——"

"Don't," Calvin answered. "There isn't time. I came here to help you."

"Oh," she said, "that's one way of putting it."

"Don't," Calvin Gates repeated. "I do want to help you, Miss Dillaway. I'm afraid you're in trouble."

The confusion and the anger had left her face and her brown eyes grew wider.

"Go ahead," she answered. "What is it, Gates?" And Calvin told her bluntly because it was the only way to tell it.

"Your Russian has been murdered," he told her. "A political murder I think—by the police."

She walked toward him and rested her hand on his arm and her lips trembled. It was an ugly enough moment, but he was only conscious that she trusted him and that she had touched his arm.

"Murdered," she whispered. "How do you know that?"

"I know it," he answered, "because I saw him die."

She reached her hand toward him again, and he held it in his for a moment.

"It's going to be all right," he said.

Then she drew her hand away and it was exactly as though a door had closed between them, for her composure had come back—that same casual mask which he had seen on the train.

"I want you to listen," Calvin Gates went on. "I want you to try to trust me and do what I tell you. Do you think you can?"

"Yes," she said, "I think I can. I don't know you very well." And she smiled. It was a poor attempt at a smile. "Do you have to be so dramatic, Gates?"

Calvin Gates looked back at her soberly.

"I'm sorry," he began, "to have broken in here."

"Good heavens," said Miss Dillaway, "let's not go over that again. What are you staring at, Gates?"

"It's you," said Calvin Gates, "you're beautiful."

"Well, you needn't look so surprised," said Miss Dillaway. "You didn't come here to tell me that."

"No," he said, "I didn't. The Russian was killed on account of that cigarette case, the one he gave you, the one you put in your purse. They know you have it, Miss Dillaway. You must get rid of it at once."

She pushed her hair back from her forehead again.

"Why should he be killed on account of that?" she asked.

Calvin Gates shook his head. "You'll have to take my word for it," he said. "There isn't any time to find out why. I'm asking you to give me your purse with that cigarette case right away."

"But why?" she asked him. "Aren't you going to tell me why?"

"Not now," said Calvin Gates.

Miss Dillaway put her head to one side. "But why should I?" she asked.

"Because I'm asking you," Calvin said, "and I'm asking you to do it quickly, because you need help worse than you ever did in your life."

She stood there for a moment small and straight in her light green gown, like a painting in a gallery, and then she smiled.

"My knight," she said, "my knight in armor."

The effect of her remark on Calvin was not agreeable.

"I wish you wouldn't call me that," he said. "You can either give me your purse or not."

"I'm sorry, Gates," she said, and her voice was suddenly contrite. "I'm generally able to look out for myself, you know. Suppose I give you my purse, then what?"

"In half an hour I want you to ring your bell," Calvin told her. "Open your door and scream if you want to. Say a man broke into your room and snatched your purse. Say that you think he was a Russian. Make all the noise you like, I'll be there to help."

She looked at him and said nothing.

"Well," said Calvin Gates, "will you do it, or won't you?"

When she answered all her embarrassment had gone.

"I never thought I'd do a thing like this," she said: "do what I'm told without knowing why. I don't know anything about you. I don't know why I do it. Are you really going on that expedition, Gates? I'm all alone here. Are you really being honest?"

"I'm going to leave with you for Peiping tomorrow," Calvin told her.

Miss Dillaway put her hand under the pillow of her bed, and drew out her worn black leather handbag. Now that she was in her green gown the handbag looked incongruous.

"I'll take my money and my passport out," she said.

"Please don't," said Calvin Gates. "That's what you are to make the row about, because your money and your passport are gone. Don't speak about the cigarette case until they ask you." He took the bag out of her hand.

"Remember," he said, "in half an hour."

Miss Dillaway nodded.

"I don't know anything about it," she said, "but I suppose I ought to thank you, Gates." There was an added touch of color in her cheeks and her eyes were bright. "Take care of yourself, will you, Gates? I don't want to miss you on the train tomorrow."

CHAPTER 7

TAKE CARE OF YOURSELF, GATES.

Those casual words had an ironical sound when he stopped to think of them.

"Yes," his thoughts were whispering, "I don't much care what happens. I might as well go out this way as any other."

He was under no illusions, since Mr. Moto's implications, though gentle, had been precise. It was in Mr. Moto's power to make him disappear as completely as the

46

man whom he had spoken to that night. He lay in his bed five minutes later, listening, occasionally looking at his watch, but there was no sound to indicate that the hotel was not asleep. It was up to Miss Dillaway to do the rest, and he wondered if she would. As it happened, she did it very well, better than he had hoped.

First he heard the lift moving and a pounding of steps on the stairs. Then he heard Miss Dillaway's voice in the hall.

"Doesn't anyone hear my bell?" she was calling. "Can't someone come up here? Help!"

Calvin Gates lay still and listened. Doors were opening and a murmur of voices grew louder, but Miss Dillaway's voice rose above them angrily.

"What sort of a place do you call this?" he heard Miss Dillaway saying. "He came into my room. He snatched my purse and ran. Isn't there anybody here who can understand English? Aren't you going to do anything?"

The murmur of voices continued as Calvin Gates got slowly out of bed and put on his trench coat and opened his door. At the far end of the long corridor half a dozen people had gathered. The gray-haired hotel manager was there, still in his frock coat, some hotel boys, and Mr. Moto, and some Japanese men in kimonos.

"Please, madam," the hotel manager was saying, "please be calm."

"Calm!" Miss Dillaway snapped at him. "He came right into my room. I want my passport and my letters of credit and my traveler's checks." Then she noticed Calvin Gates.

"Hello," she said, "it's time you woke up. You're an American, aren't you? Aren't you going to help me? Someone stole my purse."

"Your purse?" said Calvin Gates. "I'm sorry."

"Sorry!" Miss Dillaway said. "Everybody says he's sorry. Aren't you going to do something? You're a man, aren't you? I've lost my purse."

"Now wait a minute," said Calvin Gates, "I don't see how——" But Mr. Moto interrupted him.

"Please," said Mr. Moto, and he looked disturbed and

puzzled. "Everyone is looking. When did it happen, please?"

"He was in here just three minutes ago," Miss Dillaway cried "I began calling as soon as he ran out. He ran down the stairs—down there."

"Downstairs?" Mr. Moto said soothingly. "Make no doubt he will be found. Did you lock your door, please?"

"Don't ask idiotic questions," Miss Dillaway said. "Of course I locked my door. But any fool could pick a lock like that, and there wasn't any bolt. He woke me up when he was reaching under the pillow."

"Oh yes," said Mr. Moto. "So sorry to ask stupid questions. What did he look like, please?"

"Look like?" Miss Dillaway repeated. "I can't see in the dark."

"So silly of me," Mr. Moto murmured; "so you did not see." Before she could answer, he turned and looked at Calvin Gates.

"He wasn't tall, and he wasn't Japanese. He spoke to me," Miss Dillaway said.

"Ah, he spoke to you?" Mr. Moto brightened. "Oh? What did he tell you, please?"

"What do you think?" Miss Dillaway answered. "Do you think we talked about the weather? He told me he'd kill me if I cried out."

"Oh," said Mr. Moto, "so interesting. Thank you. Not a large man—and how did his voice sound, please?"

Miss Dillaway's answer was prompt and incisive.

"Like someone who has learned English out of a book," she said. "He wasn't English. His voice was in his throat. He might have been German, or Russian perhaps."

"Ah," said Mr. Moto, "Russian? Was there anything more, please?"

"Yes, one thing more." Calvin Gates drew in his breath, waiting for her to go on. "He had perfume on him."

Calvin Gates exhaled softly. Miss Dillaway had done better than he'd thought, Mr. Moto's eyes were bright and still and he rubbed his hands together gently.

"Thank you," he said. "What sort of perfume, please?"

"How should I know?" Miss Dillaway said. "It had musk in it, that's all."

"Ah," said Mr. Moto, "musk. Thank you so very much. I am so very, very grateful."

He paused. A voice was calling from the stairway—one of the hotel boys was running down the hall, calling something in Japanese. Mr. Moto smiled delightedly.

"Wait," said Mr. Moto. "So nice that you had patience. They have found your purse—on the stairs."

A moment later he was holding it out to her, bowing above it. There was an excited surge of Japanese voices.

"So glad," said Mr. Moto. "I hope so much it is yours."

"Yes," said Miss Dillaway, "of course it's mine. They found it on the stairs?"

Mr. Moto bowed again.

"Will you very kindly examine it, please?" he asked. "Yes. The thief must have been so frightened that he dropped it. I hope so much that everything is there."

Miss Dillaway was looking through the purse.

"Yes," she said, "everything. Why, he didn't even take my money! There's only one thing that's gone, and it doesn't matter."

"I am so very pleased." Mr. Moto drew in his breath and smiled, but it seemed to Calvin that his smile was hardly more than a courteous gesture. "What was it that did not matter?"

Miss Dillaway shrugged her shoulders.

"Just a silver cigarette case," she said. "It was given to me yesterday. I've still got one of my own. I guess I'm pretty lucky and thank you very much."

"You are so welcome," Mr. Moto said. "A silver cigarette case? What did it look like, please? We shall try so hard to find it."

"Really," said Miss Dillaway, "it doesn't amount to anything. I don't really care at all. It was Japanese work of silver inlaid with gunmetal. There were birds on it."

"Ah," said Mr. Moto, "lots of little birds? Please, you did not count them, did you?"

"Count them?" said Miss Dillaway. "Why under the sun should I count them?"

"No reason." Mr. Moto sighed. "Thank you so much."

"Thank you," said Miss Dillaway. "You've all been very kind."

"It has been such a great pleasure," said Mr. Moto. "I am sure you will not be disturbed again; so very, very sure."

"Is there anything more I can do, Miss Dillaway?" Calvin Gates asked her.

Miss Dillaway wrinkled her nose.

"More?" she answered. "I don't see that you've done anything except stand there."

Calvin Gates turned without answering and walked slowly down the hall, and Mr. Moto fell in step beside him.

"Mr. Gates," he said.

"Yes," Calvin answered.

Mr. Moto drew in his breath behind his hand.

"This is so very unfortunate. I am so very much ashamed. Everything has been so very clumsy. Now I must start all over again."

"I don't know what you're driving at," Calvin said. "I suppose someone stole that case."

"Yes," said Mr. Moto, "I think that I must kill myself if I do not find that case."

"Kill yourself?" Calvin Gates repeated.

Mr. Moto's gold teeth glittered in a polite impersonal smile.

"So sorry," he said. "A code of honor. You will say nothing about this, I hope so very much."

"I told you I wouldn't," said Calvin Gates. Mr. Moto drew a card from his pocket and wrote something on it.

"My address, please," he said. "If you hear about that case I should be so very glad if you would let me know. Have you traveled in England, Mr. Gates?"

"Yes," said Calvin Gates, "a little."

"Ha ha," said Mr. Moto, "exactly what I thought. That is where you learned to put your shoes outside your door? So very few Americans lean to put their shoes outside their doors at night. I hope that you will have such a very pleasant journey."

CHAPTER 8

AT NOON THE NEXT DAY Calvin Gates walked across the lobby to the desk to pay his bill. He still did not know whether he had been clever or not the night before, but he knew that he had done a dangerous thing and for the first time in a long while he was not thinking about himself. He was learning that a determined urbanity was one of Japan's heaven-sent gifts and that all which was ugly or difficult was repressed by power of will. The night was lost in a sunny morning. Memory had banished in the winelike air that set Calvin Gates's nerves tingling in a staccato sort of rhythm, like the hoofbeats of the horses which drew those ancient Russian droshkies across the square outside.

The manager bowed and smiled and handed him his bill.

"Breakfast is included," the manager said. "The porter will take you to the train and find you seats. It is best to leave please in three quarters of an hour. I hope that you were comfortable last night?"

Calvin put his change carefully in his pocket. His brownish freckled face was as imperturbable as the face in front of him.

"A very comfortable night," he said. "You have such a nice hotel."

"So glad," the manager said, "thank you." And that was all.

Calvin Gates leaned an elbow on the hotel desk.

"And Mr. Moto," he inquired, "is he up this morning yet?"

"So sorry," the manager said. "Mr. Moto was up early. He is gone."

"Oh," said Calvin Gates; "he is busy, I suppose?"

"Yes," the manager in his frock coat seized eagerly upon the explanation. "He is busy."

All the past was lost in the imperturbable present. Cal-

51

vin Gates was thinking that the Japanese had a good many impossible things to explain in the last few years, but that they always faced the facts with that same smile. They explained their adventure in Manchukuo in that same manner, and their infiltration beyond the Chinese Wall. Like Mr. Moto they were always very busy—always busy, a nervous, vital race.

There was a tramp of feet outside on the square, that indescribable sound of a body of men marching at route order, and he stepped to the hotel door to watch. A battalion of infantry was moving by in iron helmets, weighted down under complete field equipment, out perhaps for a practice march or possibly for something else. The new conquerors of Manchuria were moving across the square, squat, woodeny boys who were evidently an ordinary sight, to be accepted wearily as an old story by the people. First there had been the Manchus, then the Russians, and then the Old Marshal, and then the Japanese. He was still watching them when Miss Dillaway stepped out the door and stood beside him.

"Hello," she said. "Do you want to play soldier?" Her head was tilted toward him.

"Hello," he answered. "It looks as though there's going to be a war."

Miss Dillaway wrinkled her nose.

"Suppose you get down to earth," she said. "It isn't any of our business, is it? We've got half an hour before we leave for the station. Suppose you tell me exactly what happened last night."

"Not here," said Calvin Gates. "We're probably being watched."

"All right," said Miss Dillaway, "if you like to pretend that you're in a dime novel."

She did not bring up the subject again until they were on the train seated side by side.

"Now tell me about last night," she said.

Calvin Gates folded his hands across his knee. "The less you know about it the better," he answered. "It was true what I told you last night. He was killed."

Miss Dillaway gave a short, unmusical laugh.

"All right," she said. "Have it your own way. It might

52

be better if you told me. Didn't I behave all right last night?"

"No one could have done better," said Calvin Gates.

She leaned nearer to him so that their shoulders touched.

"Where's that cigarette case?" she said.

"It doesn't matter," he said.

"Oh yes, it does," she answered. "You'd better tell me or I won't stop talking."

"It's in my pocket," Calvin said. She was startled. Her eyes were suddenly wide and incredulous.

"Don't say any more," said Calvin Gates.

Miss Dillaway's voice was low.

"You don't care much what happens to you, do you, Gates?" she said.

Calvin Gates smiled at her. "No," he answered, "not very much."

Miss Dillaway squared her shoulders.

"I knew there was something the matter with you the first time I saw you. What did you keep it for?"

"No good reason," he said. "He asked me to, that's all."

"Who?"

"The Russian."

"Oh he did, did he?" said Miss Dillaway. "Well, why did you do what he asked you?"

Calvin Gates frowned and looked at the freckles on the back of his hands.

"Well," said Miss Dillaway, "you haven't answered, Gates."

He turned to her again as though he had forgotten her and her question.

"Frankly, it's a little hard to answer," he said, "but I suppose you ought to have some sort of explanation."

"Thank you," said Miss Dillaway, "that's very thoughtful of you, Gates."

He ignored her remark and looked straight ahead of him, speaking slowly.

"I'm not so worried about the Japanese," he said, "it's the others. There must be some others to whom this thing is very important. It's some form of a message of course. Those others may still think you have it. That's why I'm keeping it, Miss Dillaway. In case there is any trouble, it might be better to have it than not. Of course I may be wrong."

Miss Dillaway glanced at him sideways.

"So you're doing this for me. Is that true?" she said.

"Partly," he nodded slowly.

"Well, you needn't," said Miss Dillaway. "You'd better throw it out the window, Gates."

"Perhaps," said Calvin Gates, "but I'm not sure. They might not believe that we'd thrown it out the window. If they did believe, they might think that we understood about it. I think it's better keeping it, a great deal better."

"Don't you think," inquired Miss Dillaway, and her words were sweetly deliberate, "you are taking a good deal on yourself?"

"Perhaps," Calvin Gates agreed. "We're rather in the dark. Perhaps nothing will happen at all, but I think you need some help, Miss Dillaway."

"I haven't asked you for help, have I?" Miss Dillaway inquired.

"No," said Calvin Gates.

Miss Dillaway's color grew higher and she sat up straighter and clasped her hands tightly together. She looked sideways at him and started to speak and paused, and finally her voice had a curious note.

"You aren't doing this because you're attracted to me, are you, Gates? You can't be, because you've hardly seen me."

He was surprised by the abruptness of her question and surprised because her assurance was gone, but he was startled by his own answer. He had intended to speak lightly and instead he was being serious.

"I saw you last night," he said.

She turned away from him and looked out the window.

"You can't be doing this just because you saw me with my hair down my back," Miss Dillaway said.

"I'm not sure," said Calvin Gates.

Miss Dillaway turned back from the window.

"Don't try to be gallant, Gates," she said. "That sort of thing is stuff and nonsense. Of course I wouldn't have

54

asked that question if I'd even thought that you'd pretend to take it seriously."

"Why is it nonsense," Calvin asked her, "to look the way you did last night?"

He felt her shoulder beside his stiffen and her lips closed tight.

"It's nonsense," she said, "because it makes trouble. I have my work to do and I don't want to be bothered. I don't want to be bothered when I'm traveling by myself."

"So you put on a disguise," said Calvin Gates; "is that what you mean?"

Miss Dillaway looked surprised. "It isn't what I mean exactly. I like to be judged for what I am, not for the way I look, and now you say because you saw me in a green kimono— It's rather silly, Gates."

"Is it?" Calvin asked her. "I don't see why."

"I'll tell you why," said Miss Dillaway: "because you're a romanticist, Gates. You're a type which ought to be extinct—the knight errant type. Anyone in a green negligee would do. You don't care who's inside it. You only care for the idea."

"No," said Calvin Gates, "that isn't true."

Miss Dillaway's eyes sparkled. "Oh yes, it's true," she said. "Any lady in any wrapper, Gates. I wish you'd give me back that cigarette case, Gates. I can manage it just as well as you can. I don't even know who you are. Why should I be obliged to you?"

"I'm not asking you to be obliged," said Calvin Gates.

"Oh yes, you are," Miss Dillaway answered, "but you never even thought of it that way."

Calvin Gates stood up.

"Just the same I'm going to keep it," he said, "whether you like it or not. You're a funny person, Miss Dillaway. First I like you and then I don't. I may be a romanticist, but I'm not afraid of life."

She looked startled and then she smiled.

"No one ever said that to me before," she said. "I'm not afraid of life."

"You're running away from it," he told her. "You're running away from it now."

"Then so are you," said Miss Dillaway tartly. "You're

running away from something, at any rate. I don't understand you, Gates."

"It doesn't really matter," Calvin said.

The observation car was almost a copy of the one they had left the day before, and he sat in another of the wicker chairs staring out of the window. The remarks he had made to Miss Dillaway afforded him no satisfaction. Instead he was obsessed by a lonely sense of his own futility. He was alone again in a world of Orientals, of Japanese army officers and Japanese businessmen. Outside the country had grown level and there were faint yellowish dust clouds on the horizon, and the same mud villages and blue-clad laborers.

It must have been an hour later when Miss Dillaway entered the car and seated herself in a vacant chair beside him.

"Hello," she said, "are you angry with me, Gates?"

"No," he told her.

"I'm glad you're not," Miss Dillaway said, "because I don't like it there alone. People keep watching me."

"Who?" he asked. "Anyone in particular?"

Miss Dillaway shook her head.

"No one in particular, just the train guard and the train boy. I'd rather be with you. You're better, Gates."

"It's kind of you to say so," he answered.

She wrinkled her nose and sniffed.

"I'm sorry if I've been disagreeable. It's just the way I am, I guess. We can't help being what we are."

"No," he answered, "I don't suppose we can."

"If I could, I'd change right away," she said.

"So would I," he answered.

"The trouble is we just have to keep being what we are unless something changes us. Do you suppose anything will ever change us, Gates?"

Calvin Gates smiled and forgot that they were in Manchuria.

"Probably for the worse," he said.

She laughed and held out her hand. "You're not so bad," she answered. "Let's go into the dining car and have a drink. I'll match you for who pays."

"No," he said, "I'll buy it."

"I'm not being ladylike, am I?" she said. "I told you we couldn't change. I'll match you, I can't help it, Gates."

Nevertheless Miss Dillaway had changed. She was no longer concealing her personality from him or trying to act a part and it must have been an effort for her to go as far as that. It pleased him, more than he thought was possible, that she had surrendered to some intuition and, without knowing who he was or what, had given him her friendship. It made him happy even though he knew that there would only be one ending. It would be better to tell her something about himself beforehand; it would be the only honorable way, since they were friends, but he hesitated.

"I know I'm disagreeable when I'm traveling, Gates," she said confidingly. "My temper always goes to pieces when I'm worried, and I say any amount of things that I'm sorry for afterwards. I'm frightened most of the time when I'm on these trips and I don't want anyone to know it. It's not as bad with you. I'm really having a nice time."

"So am I," said Calvin Gates; "the first time in a long while, and you're the only reason for it, Miss Dillaway."

"You'd better call me Dillaway," she said. "My first name is Sylvia, and I don't like it much. My friends all call me Dillaway. I may as well warn you, I'm as likely as not to snap your head off before we get to Peiping, and you'll probably want to choke me. You should have seen the way I tore into poor Boris. At the customs' shed." She stopped and caught her breath. "Aren't you going to tell me what happened to him, Gates? How did he——"

Calvin interrupted her and spoke quickly. If she had to know, and it would probably be better if she did, he wished to make that whole ugly affair casual and literal.

"He came to my room to ask me to take that cigarette case he gave you. He was shot while he was talking to me. A man came in and shot him from the balcony. It isn't pleasant, but I suppose you ought to know. Then Mr. Moto came and took the whole thing in hand."

"That little man?" she said.

"Yes, it had something to do with the police. What do you know about that Russian?"

"Nothing," she answered. "I asked for a courier at the hotel."

Calvin Gates nodded.

"What do you think he was doing?"

"Carrying a message," she answered promptly. "He was frightened in the train. What do you suppose that thing's about? Have you looked at it?"

"No," he said, "but I think he had told someone else that he had given it to you. He had all evening to make arrangements."

Calvin Gates folded his hands carefully, unfolded them again and laid them palm down upon each knee.

"I've been trying most of last night to figure it out. Granted that it is some sort of message, it's a very important one or they wouldn't have killed the man who was carrying it. If it is a message it is probably going to someone near where we are going, but after that I'm puzzled. Whoever sent the message certainly wanted it delivered."

"Well, that's obvious," Miss Dillaway said.

"The next point is not so obvious," he answered. "Moto wants it delivered too. In fact, he told me so."

"Now wait a minute," said Miss Dillaway. "This can't be right. If he wanted the message delivered why should they have killed Boris?"

Calvin Gates moved his shoulders uneasily and drummed his fingers on his knee.

"I gathered that it was a mistake," he explained slowly. "I don't think Mr. Moto liked it. He seemed to want to have things go smoothly. At any rate he told me so."

Miss Dillaway looked at him hard.

"It seems to me that he told you quite a good deal."

"Yes." Calvin Gates looked back at her. "He told me a good deal."

Miss Dillaway wrinkled her forehead.

"You're not being frank, Gates," she said. "Why should he have told you that much?"

Calvin Gates felt his fingers grip his knees tightly because the time had come. In another minute she would know that he was not a nice young man and certainly not a proper person for a friend. He was surprised how much he valued her friendship and how much he wanted her to think well of him, now that she would not and could not, because she was honest, devastatingly honest.

"Because Mr. Moto has something on me," he said. He spoke slowly because every word hurt him. "He thought he could make me let you carry that cigarette case for him. I think I fooled him last night. He doesn't know who's got it now."

She looked at him startled, exactly the way he thought that she would look.

"How could a little Japanese have anything on you?" she asked. "I don't see how it's possible."

Calvin spoke more slowly and his mouth was grim and straight.

"I may as well tell you I'm a notorious character, Miss Dillaway," he said. He tried to speak casually, but his voice was strained and discordant. "I am a fugitive from justice, Miss Dillaway." He saw her start and stare at him exactly as he knew she would and he went on grimly. If there was anything between them, it would be better to have it over.

"I like you well enough so that I'm blunt," he went on. "I found out last night that Mr. Moto knew everything about me. He's a Japanese agent. The whole nation seems to be alive with them. He threatened to turn me over to the authorities, if I said anything about last night and if I didn't let you carry that cigarette case. He's smart, but maybe I was smarter. You haven't got it now."

Her brown eyes had the same look that he had seen back at the hotel. He saw her clasp and unclasp her hands and when she spoke her voice was low and frightened.

"I generally know about people," she said. "I knew that something was the matter with you. What did you do back home, Gates?"

"I forged a check," he said. He had meant to keep his voice low, but instead it was harsh and bitter. He saw her start when he said it, but her eyes were still and deep.

"You did it on account of some girl," she said. "You did, Gates, didn't you?"

He stared out of the window before he answered. The train was moving rapidly across a level country which gave an impression of another age, with interminable cultivated fields, surrounding mud villages each behind a high mud wall. It was as though the clock had been turned back a thousand years, and there he was wretched in the present.

"Not exactly," he said slowly. "She was my first cousin and I always disliked her very much. It doesn't really matter. The point is I'm a forger. The point is I'm all washed up. Maybe it's just as well I told you. Forgers aren't popular with anyone, I guess. Keep your checkbook away from me, Miss Dillaway."

He leaned back in his wicker chair and stared straight ahead of him, uncomfortable at her silence, because her silence was worse than words. He was waiting for her to speak, bracing himself to hear what she might say. He saw her glance at him sideways.

"Do you still want to match me for a drink?" she said.

His face grew bright red underneath his tan and freckles. He had never known that he could be moved so deeply by anything that anyone could say to him.

"Do you mean you still want to talk to me?" he asked. "I haven't been joking, Dillaway."

Miss Dillaway wrinkled her nose.

"See if you've got a coin in your pocket," she said. "You've got clumsy hands for a forger, Gates." And that was all she said.

He put his hand in his pocket and drew out a Japanese coin with a hole through the middle of it.

"The trouble with it is," he said, "that it hasn't got any heads or tails."

Miss Dillaway laughed.

"You can't make heads or tails of anything in Japan," she answered, "that why. I've got an American fifty-cent piece. Wait a minute."

She was opening her handbag and the train was slowing down beside one of those incongruous, half-European looking stations, built of neat gray brick with a gray tiled roof. Beyond it, perhaps half a mile away, he could see a town, larger than any they had passed, with somber gray brick walls and an arched gate with battlements on either side and with a curved roof structure above it. A line of two-wheeled carts drawn by chunky little horses moved into the town, and behind them came a row of donkeys laden with fagots. The train guard was drawn up on the station platform and their bayonets glittered in the summer sun, partly concealing a group of Chinese country people who stood behind them, watching incuriously. The train was slowing down and a food vendor with tea and rice and spaghetti was running beside it, calling in a plaintive singsong voice.

"It looks like a big town," said Calvin Gates, "I wonder what it is."

"It looks dirty," said Miss Dillaway. "Here's the fifty-cent piece, Gates. Look at the barbed wire and sandbags. You'd better call it, Gates. What do you want, heads or tails?"

"Heads," he said.

Miss Dillaway slapped the coin on the back of her hand.

"You lose, Gates," she said. "It's tails. Why look, what's happening now?"

The rear door of the observation car had opened and a young Japanese subaltern entered, followed by two soldiers with their rifles with bayonets at port. The officer was hardly out of his teens and his expression was eager and ambitious. He was holding a piece of paper in his hand which he consulted scrupulously, and finally looked at Calvin Gates. Calvin put his hand in his pocket and looked back at the officer.

"I'm afraid," he said, "Mr. Moto's guessed I've got that cigarette case."

Miss Dillaway pulled his sleeve.

"Then give it to me, Gates," she said.

Calvin Gates did not look at her, but continued to examine the officer.

"It's too late now," he answered. "I'm afraid we'd better say good-by, Miss Dillaway. You've been nice to me—much too nice."

The officer halted before Calvin Gates and spoke very slowly in English, accenting each syllable tonelessly and conscientiously, like a student who has learned the language from a phrase book.

"Good afternoon," the officer said. "Please, you come with me."

Calvin smiled, but the officer did not smile.

"Where?" Calvin asked.

The officer paused, laboring hard with the eccentricities of an unknown tongue.

"Arise off your sit, please," he said. "Go off the train with me at once."

Calvin Gates rose.

"Well," he said, "good-by, Miss Dillaway."

Miss Dillaway had risen also.

"If you're getting off this train," she said, "I'm getting off with you."

"No." Calvin Gates's tone was sharp. "You're doing no such thing. This is my party, and it wouldn't do you any good, but if you see Dr. Gilbreth up there, I wish you'd tell him that I forged that check."

"But Gates,—" she clung tight to his arm,—"what are they going to do with you?"

His expression was not entirely agreeable. He stood a head and shoulders above the little officer.

"It doesn't make a bit of difference," he said.

"But they don't even understand English," Miss Dillaway cried.

"It doesn't make any difference," Calvin Gates repeated. "Good-by, Miss Dillaway."

He walked toward the rear platform with the officer beside him and the soldiers just behind.

"Gates!" Miss Dillaway called after him, but he did not answer. In fact he only half heard her, for he seemed to have moved from the train already and from all that country.

CHAPTER 9

OUT ON THE STATION PLATFORM, warm in the late June sunlight, the crowd of chattering, blue-clad Chinese rustics moved hastily aside. He had a glimpse of rolls of bedding and dilapidated baggage, broad dull faces and dull staring eyes. The air was heavy with the odors of coal smoke, and of dough cakes, spaghetti and curiously varnished chickens that were exposed for sale.

"This way please," the officer said.

He was conducted into a bare and dirty room with a bench along one side of a wall, made greasy by others who had leaned against it waiting. Some soldiers sitting on the bench looked at him and looked away.

"Please," the lieutenant said, "you sit." And Calvin Gates sat down. At the end of the room, behind a plain wooden table, was seated a sallow, sickly-looking officer, whose eyes blinked from behind heavy lensed spectacles. In a sharp querulous voice he interrogated a tall, muscular Chinese peasant, clad in nothing but slippers and blue trousers. A Japanese guard whose head reached hardly above the shoulder of the Chinese stood beside him. Without knowing the language, Calvin Gates could understand what was happening by the intonation and by the repetition of syllables. The Chinese was denying something doggedly and stolidly as the officer pressed the question. The lieutenant who had brought Calvin in glanced toward the table and sat down.

"Will not take long," he said.

The voice of the officer suddenly grew sharper, and the guard standing on tiptoe struck the Chinese across the face. The lieutenant glanced sideways at Calvin Gates.

"Bad man," he said; "naughty man, a bandit."

Calvin could see the train through the open window, still waiting, and he wondered why it was delayed. He finally leaned his back against the wall where so many others had leaned before him and drew a travel folder from his pocket, a descriptive pamphlet of Mukden which he had found at the hotel. The lieutenant turned toward him quickly.

"I can read, can't I?" Calvin asked.

"Yes," the lieutenant said, "oh yes."

The writer of the pamphlet had been like the lieutenant, a student not wholly familiar with the English language, and thus the words and tenses of that folder progressed with a breathless, eager inaccuracy:—

MANCHURIAN INCIDENT AND NORTH BARRACKS. At 10:30 P.M. on the 18th of Sept. 1931, the Manchurian Incident was started by the insolent explosion of the railway track at Liutiso kou between Mukden and Wen-kuan-tun stations of the South Manchurian Railway, which was executed by the Chinese regular soldiers. After the explosion the Chinese soldiers attempted to flee themselves in the direction of the North Barracks, but just then they were found by the Japanese railway guards under Lieutenant Kawamoto, who were patrolling the place on duty. Suddenly the both sides exchanged the bullets and the Japanese made a fierce pursuit after them. On the next moment, the Chinese forces of some three companies appeared from the thickly growed Kaolian field near the North Barracks, against which the Japanese opposed bravely and desperately, meantime despatching the urgent report to their commander. The skirmish developed speedily and the Japanese troop was compelled to make a violent attack upon the North Barracks where were stationed the brigade of Major-General Wang-icho, to lead the conditions favorable. After several hours of fierce battle, the barracks fell completely into the hand of the Japanese forces.

On the other hand, the Japanese regiment in Mukden rose in concert with the railway guards in the midnight of the same day and succeeded in occupying the walled town, East Barracks, Aerodrome etc., fighting till 2:00 P.M. of the following day with the reinforcement of the other regiments stationed at Liao-yang and Hai-chang.

The North Barracks is opened to the public inspection, and can be reached in 20 minutes by motor car from S.M.R. Mukden Station.

The words of that short account contained an indirect significance, which revealed something of the spirit of Japan. They conveyed an inevitable sense of going somewhere and a sense of destiny. That incident had happened a good many years back but it had repeated itself since and would repeat itself again. In a small way Calvin felt its elements before him in that ugly fly-blown room, illustrated by the heavy Chinese prisoner and the diminutive guard beside him.

The guard gave the prisoner a prod with the butt of his rifle, and the man walked away, beyond the imagination of Calvin Gates, impassively, without fear or anger, with a patient resignation and a poise beyond Calvin's understanding. The lieutenant looked after him complacently.

"Naughty man," he said. "Will be shot. Get off your sit please. The officer will see you."

The sallow Japanese behind the table drummed the tips of his fingers on the boards and spoke sharply in the same querulous, scolding tones. The lieutenant twitched at Calvin's sleeve and the two walked over to the table. That twitch on the sleeve, gentle though it had been, was almost a discourtesy. He knew that his resentment was not childish, because he was already learning something of the importance of personal dignity and something of that Oriental term, "face," which no European can entirely define.

"Take your hand off me," he said to the lieutenant. It was a small matter but he knew that the soldiers and the two officers in the room understood him. Although the lieutenant's face was blank, he understood. The officer behind the table rose from his chair and spoke again in Japanese. The lieutenant drew in his breath, bowed to Calvin Gates and spoke in his schoolbook English.

"Sorry," he said. "Excuse."

Not entirely to Calvin's surprise, but to his relief, the officer behind the table spoke in excellent English.

"Excuse him," he said. "You are Mr. Gates I think. I am the colonel here in command of the district. There was a telegram about you."

The colonel spoke in Japanese again and the lieutenant saluted and gave an order. There was a scuffling noise of feet which made Calvin Gates look behind him. The lieutenant and the soldiers were leaving the room. The colonel watched them go and did not speak until he and Gates were alone.

The light from the window glittered on the colonel's glasses and he stood stiffly behind the table.

"It is a telegram from a gentleman who knows you, a

65

very important man who shares my political beliefs. His name is Mr. Moto."

"I thought it was," said Calvin Gates. "About a cigarette case, is it?"

There was no longer any doubt that Mr. Moto knew where the cigarette case was, and now Calvin knew that Mr. Moto had guessed even before he had left the hotel at Mukden. He remembered Mr. Moto's polite remark about the shoes outside the door; it was then that Mr. Moto had guessed.

"Yes," the colonel said. "He is asking to be sure if you have a cigarette case with little birds upon it."

"He is right," said Calvin Gates. "I suppose you want it, Colonel."

"Yes," the colonel said. "So sorry to trouble you, but I must see it."

Calvin reached in his inside pocket, but the colonel stopped him.

"Be careful," he said. "Step to the corner here in case someone is looking through the window. Now you may take it out. Thank you."

The colonel took the cigarette case in both hands and bowed. He turned it over carefully, opened it and closed it.

"Thank you," the colonel said suddenly. "Thank you so very much. You may take it back now, Mr. Gates."

"What—" said Calvin Gates. "You want me to take it back? What for? I don't want it."

Before he answered the colonel smiled at him as though they both knew something which had better not be expressed.

"Of course," the colonel said. "That is what Mr. Moto has directed. He only wished to be sure all was in order. I am so sure that you understand."

"Understand what?" Calvin asked him.

The colonel smiled again.

"Of course," the colonel said, "Mr. Moto has explained. It is an honor to meet a friend of Mr. Moto. They will bring some tea if you will join me, please. The other instructions will not take a moment."

Calvin Gates felt his thoughts move dizzily, but his instinct told him that it was better to show no astonishment.

"Here is the tea and a chair for you," the colonel said. "This is so very important. Will you please sit down?"

Two soldiers had entered as the colonel was speaking, one carrying a chair and another a blue-and-white teapot.

The colonel raised his teacup.

"Mr. Moto is a very able man," he said.

"Yes," said Calvin, "a very able man."

"And he forgets nothing," the colonel said.

"No," said Calvin, "I don't believe he forgets anything."

"So you must listen," the colonel said, "as I speak for Mr. Moto." The colonel lowered his voice.

"There was a long telegram. Mr. Moto wanted you told that others know you have the case. I hope you understand."

"Oh," said Calvin Gates, "some others know, do they?"

"Yes." The colonel sipped his tea. "It is so unfortunate. Mr. Moto is afraid that they may try to get it. He asked that you be very careful. You must not let it be stolen. You are not to give it away until you reach Kalgan. A man there will ask for it. His name is Mr. Holtz. Mr. Moto is most anxious that Mr. Holtz should have it."

"He didn't say anything more?" asked Calvin Gates.

"Just one thing more," the colonel said. "He wanted me to say that the others understand you are Mr. Moto's friend, and that is dangerous."

The colonel sipped his tea and the light glittered on his glasses.

"He is sorry that it is so dangerous for you. Have you a weapon, Mr. Gates?"

Calvin Gates shook his head and the colonel opened the drawer of the table.

"You see," he said, "Mr. Moto thinks of everything." He reached in the drawer and drew out an automatic pistol. "There," the colonel said; "I hope so much that you will not have to use it, and here is an extra clip of cartridges. Mr. Moto thinks of everything, does he not?"

Calvin took the pistol in the palm of his hand, examined it for a moment and slipped it into his coat pocket.

"Yes," he said a little vaguely, "Mr. Moto thinks of everything. Look here, Colonel, you'd better take this cigarette case. I don't want it."

The colonel raised his cup delicately and sipped his tea before he answered.

"Mr. Moto was afraid of that," he said. "It will do no good to give the case away. The others know you have it. They will try to get it any any rate. Mr. Moto wants you to keep it now. It is the best way he knows of having it delivered."

"Suppose I refuse?" Calvin asked him. "I don't want to be mixed up in this."

"Please." The colonel raised his hand. "You are so involved already. I do not like to threaten. You do not want to go to military prison. You might stay there very long."

"Oh," said Calvin, "that's it."

"Yes," the colonel answered. "I think that you had much rather get back upon the train. You see the train is waiting."

Calvin Gates glanced out the window. The train was waiting and the colonel was waiting also. Although his thoughts were undefined and clouded by uncertainty, he was beginning to understand what had happened, and the brain of Mr. Moto was behind it. For some reason of his own, ever since they had first met on the boat, Mr. Moto had been waiting while one thing led to another.

Calvin Gates folded his hands across his knee and he felt as he had before, like a slow-witted barbarian who was uncouthly trying to understand unknown complexities.

"Why does Mr. Moto want me to carry this thing?" he asked.

The colonel smiled as though he had explained everything, though he had not expected the abruptness of the question. He replaced his glasses carefully on the wide bridge of his nose and studied Calvin carefully through the lenses.

"There is no reason to explain," the colonel said. "Mr. Moto wishes this delivered to the right person, and he wishes no one to be suspicious. He is sure that you can do it."

The colonel smiled as though he had explained everything.

"He says he wants you to be comfortable and to have a happy journey."

Calvin Gates got to his feet and shook his head.

"He's wrong," he said. "I won't do it."

The colonel rose also.

"You are making a great mistake," he said. "Excuse me, please." He raised his voice and called something in his own language.

The soldier opened the door so quickly that Calvin was sure that he had been waiting for the order. He opened the door and stood aside, and Calvin heard a voice he recognized. It was the lieutenant speaking.

"You come in please," the lieutenant said; and Miss Dillaway was standing in the doorway. Her chin was high and her eyes were snapping angrily.

"Hello, Gates," she said. "What have they been doing to you? That soldier wouldn't let me come in."

The colonel spoke before Calvin Gates could answer.

"So sorry, madam," he said. "You must stay, I think."

Calvin Gates spoke quickly.

"Wait a minute," he said. "She has nothing to do with it."

"So sorry," the colonel said, "she must stay here too, unless, of course, you change your mind."

"What's he talking about?" asked Miss Dillaway.

Calvin Gates shrugged his shoulders.

"It's all right," he said. "I'll take it along—if that's the way it is."

The colonel smiled and bowed. "Thank you," he said, "that is so much better."

"And you haven't got anything more to tell me?" Calvin asked.

"No," said the colonel. He held out his hand. "Good-by. Nothing more to tell you, Mr. Gates."

As they crossed the station platform Miss Dillaway touched his arm.

"What happened?" she asked. "What have they been doing to you, Gates? What have we gotten into?"

Calvin Gates looked grimly at the train and pressed his

lips together. There was no need to tell her about that scene in the station, no need that she should be alarmed.

"Just passport trouble," he said. "Just questions."

Miss Dillaway laughed shortly.

"Well," she said. "You didn't think I was going to go on without you, did you? I came out to get you. I'm glad it's only about a passport. I was afraid it was something else. If anything happens, I'm going to stop your being a hero, Gates." And then her smile died away as she glanced up at him; his face was set and hard.

"I hope to heaven you can," he said.

CHAPTER 10

THE SUN MOVED with the hours of the afternoon in its arc across a warm blue sky where a few thin grayish clouds were floating. It moved deliberately with the hours until it was so low over the limitless rolling plain that the light became benign and soft and the horizon assumed a reddish hue that was reflected on the clouds, making them shell pink and purple. The waning light softened the harsh outlines and made the walled towns that they passed mysteriously remote in a sort of timeless loneliness and endowed the whole country with an exotic portentous beauty. The train moved through that level country as surely as though the hours were pulling it. The map showed him that they were nearing the venerable city of Shan-hai-kuan by the first gate in the Great Wall of China of which he had heard so much but knew so little. The motion of the train through that changing but changeless country was almost reassuring.

Miss Dillaway looked out the window, and her face made a sharp, incisive profile, as clear and even as the profile on a coin.

"I was born in Winnetka, Illinois," Miss Dillaway said suddenly, and she was evidently speaking her thoughts aloud. "I went to Chicago University and then I went to art school. I started as a commercial artist. I had to earn my living. I'm not bad at accurate work. You've never had to earn your living, have you, Gates?"

"What made you guess that?" Calvin asked her.

"Your attitude," she answered. "You just look that way. It might have saved you trouble if you'd had to earn your living. It gets you in closer touch with facts."

"I'll have to earn my living from now on," he said.

She leaned forward under some sudden impulse and rested her hand for a moment on his knee, and that momentary contact startled him.

"What's the trouble at home?" she asked. "You'd better tell me, Gates."

"I'd rather not," he said, "if you don't mind."

It was no use. Whether he explained or not, in another day or two he would never see Miss Sylvia Dillaway again.

"All right," said Miss Dillaway. "If you don't want to talk, reach me down my sketching box, the big one on the rack there."

She sat with her sketching box on the opposite seat, counting tubes of oil paint, arranging and rearranging all the tools of her trade as if she had forgotten his existence.

She was like others he had known who could retire suddenly behind the walls of their own interests, leaving him alone. She had asked for his confidence, but he was sure that it would have done no good to have talked about himself. It was better to try to live in the present and to examine the utter strangeness of that present. When he looked out of the window there was nothing in the scene which reminded him of anything, no face or voice in the train which reminded him of anything.

In one sense that unfamiliarity was a relief, but in another it was not. He had to walk dumbly through a world he did not know, coping with a language which he did not understand, while he waited for some event to occur that he could not anticipate. Thoughtlessly, he put his hand into the side pocket of his coat and for a second what he felt there surprised him. He had almost forgotten the automatic pistol, and he still had not the remotest idea why it had been given him. Nevertheless he was glad that he had it.

Every now and then the train boy moved past him, a young uniformed Japanese, and once or twice a member of the train guard paced slowly down the aisle. Since he had boarded the train again after his interview at that station, it seemed to him that he had acquired an added importance and that there was some unspoken sort of understanding.

"Please," the train boy said slowly when it was growing dark, as though he had learned his words from a phrase book, "you get off train at Shan-hai-kuan and take sleeping train. Baggage goes to customs. Thank you please."

The sun was down and the world was gray and then it was black, and the train moved for a long while through a dark country where there was hardly ever a gleam of light. It was after nine in the evening before the train reached Shan-hai-kuan. Even if he had not known that the wall was there, it was plain that they had passed from a land of order to a land of noise and confusion. Whistles were blowing. Porters and station employees and food vendors ran beside the train, shouting and waving their arms. The whole train shed was a babble of high voices and laughter and escaping steam. Calvin Gates stared uncertainly through the smoky window.

"It looks as though everyone outside has gone crazy," he said.

Just as the train was coming to a stop and just as he had turned from the window, he saw a man of his own race thrust his way through the crowd and swing aboard. He had a glimpse of a red face and of a trench coat like his own, and then an instant later he saw the face again. A wiry, stocky European carrying a riding crop strode down the aisle toward them with a curious rolling gait. His face was ruddy from the out-of-doors, of a deep color that made his grayish eyes seem very light. He pushed past two Japanese businessmen who were starting for the door and caught sight of Calvin and Miss Dillaway.

"Hello, hello," he called. His voice was nasal and metallic and he jerked off his felt hat. "Is this by any chance Miss Dillaway?"

"Yes, it is," Miss Dillaway answered. "How do you know my name?"

She must have been as surprised as Calvin Gates to hear her name called in that remote place. The stranger's hard red face crinkled into a smile and he pulled a letter from his pocket.

"That's fine," he said, "fine. So you're the little artist lady, are you? Here's a letter from Dr. Gilbreth explaining who I am. Read it any time. My name is Hamby, miss, Captain Sam Hamby, Dardanelles, Messines Ridge. Long time ago wasn't it? Professional soldier, miss, with the Cavalry of the Prince of Ghuru Nor. I was coming down from up there on business and Dr. Gilbreth asked me to pop over here and meet you. He thought it might be easier for you. There's a spot of mix-up over in Mongolia. Don't worry, things are always mixed up in China."

Miss Dillaway read the note which he handed her and gave the red-faced stranger a smile of quick relief.

"Well," she said, "that explains everything. It's awfully kind of you, Captain Hamby, and I won't say two greenhorns like us don't need help. This is Mr. Gates, who is going up there with me, Mr. Calvin Gates from New York."

The wrinkles around Captain Hamby's lips grew deeper, and though he smiled his face grew watchful, and his eyes looked still and glassy. They reminded Calvin of the eyes of a sailor or a hunter that were accustomed to stare across great distances.

"Well, well," said Captain Hamby, "funny that Gilbreth never spoke of you. The word was that only Miss Dillaway was traveling up to Ghuru Nor."

There was something in the other's face that Calvin did not like, although he could not tell just why—something still and something watchful. His curiosity, though it was natural, aroused in Calvin a sudden resentment. Through the thoughtfulness of Dr. Gilbreth, Captain Hamby had come to take Miss Dillaway from him; and he had not wanted it just yet. It gave him a strange, unreasoning pang of jealousy which increased when he saw that Miss Dillaway looked happy and relieved.

"Dr. Gilbreth doesn't know I'm coming," Calvin said; "but I'm an old acquaintance of his. I can assure you that

73

he won't object. I've come all the way from New York on a piece of business with him."

For a second Captain Hamby's eyes maintained that curious, glassy look, and then they twinkled and his smile grew broader.

"That's fine," said Captain Hamby, "fine. Any friend of Gilbreth's a friend of mine. Capital chap, the Doctor. The more the merrier, Gates. Just leave everything to me. By jove, that's awkward," Captain Hamby paused and thrust his hands in his coat pockets, "I must have left my fags in my old kit bag and I'm perishing for a smoke. Neither of you two have a cigarette, have you?"

The question was casual enough, but there was nothing casual about Captain Hamby's light gray eyes. In the instant's hesitation that followed Calvin saw Miss Dillaway steal a sideways glance at him.

"You have a cigarette, haven't you, Gates?" she said.

Calvin produced a paper package from his pocket. A little line appeared between Captain Hamby's light eyebrows and disappeared again.

"Thanks," he said, "awfully. Deuced careless of me to forget my fags. Now you leave everything to me, I know the ropes here. I've got boys to handle the bags. We'll get through the customs before you can say knife. I'll get three compartments—Chinese sleeping train. Right? Not as good as a *wagon-lit,* but it's clean. Just leave everything to me."

Captain Hamby waved his hand toward the rear of the train in a broad, expansive gesture.

"Back there in Manchukuo—just you understand this,—" his red face wrinkled in a pantomime—"everything is dead serious; but over here—" the wrinkles curved into an exaggerated grin—"over here everything is funny, always something is funny in China. I ought to know. I've been here long enough. Just remember to keep smiling—smile, smile, smile."

Although the hard nasal voice and the pronunciation puzzled Calvin, he was beginning to comprehend that Captain Hamby was a part of that new country and as much in keeping with it as the native population. Captain Hamby was a type which Calvin had heard casually men-

74

tioned, but one which he had never seen—the Old China Hand. The analysis of Miss Dillaway went even further.

"Australian, aren't you, Captain Hamby?" she asked.

"You win, Miss Dillaway," Captain Hamby said. "Been around a bit, haven't you, to pick me out so easy? Just a noisy Aussie, and that's about the same as American, isn't it? We better pop off the train now. Just leave everything to me."

Captain Hamby jerked a window open with a quick heave of his broad shoulders and began shouting directions to the station platform in a curious mixture of English and Chinese.

"Here come the boys," he said. "The bags will be out in a minute. All you have to do is get on the other train and wait. I'll take you."

"We're certainly glad to see you," said Miss Dillaway.

"Righto," said Captain Hamby.

Two minutes later they were moving across the train shed with Captain Hamby just beside them, leading a line of four porters carrying their luggage. They were with a man who knew the ropes and who knew how to arrange everything in a way that was breezy and bullying and yet good-natured.

"Just jolly the Chinese," Captain Hamby said. "Every Chinese is a perfect gentleman. Over there—very grim; over here—comic opera."

With Captain Hamby no great effort seemed necessary. He exchanged a few sharp sentences with the Chinese Customs and then, before Calvin could even understand what formality had taken place, they were in three compartments of the Peiping train with all their baggage identified and stowed away. Captain Hamby pulled a handkerchief from his pocket, grinned and mopped his brow.

"Everything's shipshape now, eh what?" he said. "Miss Dillaway bunks there, you next, Gates, and me right beside you. I'll leave our connecting door open, Gates. And now how about a drink? Always travel with whisky in China if you know what's good for you. I'll get the boy." He opened the door and hurried into the narrow passageway outside. "Boy," Calvin could hear him shouting, "boy!"

Miss Dillaway looked after him smilingly.

"Isn't he wonderful?" she said.

"He's been a help," said Calvin Gates, but her remark gave him another twinge of jealous resentment. Miss Dillaway wrinkled her nose.

"He was a help," she said, "and a lot of help you'd have been. Don't be such a snob, Gates."

"I'm not a snob," said Calvin. "I just wonder why he asked for a cigarette."

"Why shouldn't he ask for a cigarette?" she inquired.

"No reason," Calvin answered, "but he might have had some of his own."

Captain Hamby was back with the train boy before she had time to reply. The Captain was carrying a bottle of English whisky and the train boy followed with a tray and glasses and soda.

"You can get anything you like if you know how to get it," Captain Hamby said. "Soda, Miss Dillaway? I'll take mine neat. Chin chin!"

"Chin chin," said Miss Dillaway. The sat side by side on Calvin Gates's bunk, with the glasses on a wooden hinged table in front of them. The sleeping compartment was of plain varnished wood with a single dim yellow electric bulb, but, as Captain Hamby had said, it was reasonably clean. There was a sliding glass paneled door which communicated with the passageway outside. Other passengers stared through the panel curiously and Captain Hamby pulled the shade.

"You'll get used to that," he said. "White people are a traveling circus to the Chinese. They still think our knees bend backward upcountry and that we eat babies' eyes, but they're all right, always ready for a laugh. Just pack up your troubles in your old kit bag, and smile, boys, that's the style. What's the use of worrying? It never was worth while."

"Did you say there was some trouble up where you came from?" Calvin asked.

The Captain laughed and reached for the whisky bottle.

"There's a lot of talk going around in China, always talk," he said.

76

"What sort of talk?" asked Calvin Gates.

The Captain reached for one of Calvin's cigarettes and spoke with it dangling from his lips, so that its glowing end moved jerkily with his words.

"Out here," said Captain Hamby, "you'll find out there's always trouble. There's either some war lord in the provinces, or a disbanded army running wild, or the Japanese. This time it looks like the Japanese. They're setting out to start something. Out our way it's hard to get through the wall."

"What wall?" Calvin asked him.

The Captain's light gray eyes met his with a calculating glance.

"Seems as though you're new here," the Captain said. "I'm referring to the real wall of China built before Christ. It isn't much more than a mound now but there's a gate in it outside of Kalgan, and then there comes Mongolia. It's hard to get through now. That's why Gilbreth sent me."

"Oh," said Calvin Gates, "I see. You mean the Japanese?"

Captain Hamby nodded and finished his drink.

"You can't be sure," he said and lowered his voice. "It looks as though they're pushing in again. First it was Manchuria and then it was Jehol, and then influence over Peiping. It looks like all North China this time. Another incident—of course you can never be sure. I've seen enough of this never to be sure. Someone might start shooting. Anyway, up where I live things aren't going right. Maybe I don't make myself clear."

Captain Hamby took off his felt hat and it changed him. His dark brown hair was very closely clipped and growing gray at the temples, but he looked neither young nor old. The wrinkles in his forehead and the crow's-feet about his eyes were made by wind and dust rather than by age.

"I'm sorry," he said. "I talk Chinese and Russian and Mongolian so much that I don't make myself clear in English. I come from Ghuru Nor. I'm commanding the Prince's Cavalry. The Prince is up-to-date, Prince Wu Fang at Ghuru Nor—that's his Chinese name. He's not bad, the Prince. It's a way to earn your living. Soldier of fortune—Captain Sam Hamby. Served under the Christian General and under the old marshal and the young marshal. Who wants another drink?"

Captain Hamby stared ahead of him at nothing. A whistle blew and the train had begun to move. Captain Hamby had spoken, he had explained himself perfectly, and his hard-bitten face and wiry body confirmed his speech. Miss Dillaway was looking at him with a respect that was annoying.

"You must have seen a lot," Miss Dillaway said.

"Beg pardon?" said Captain Hamby, and his glance traveled toward her out of nowhere. "Oh yes, a lot, and it's nice to see an English-speaking girl again. We're going to get on fine, Miss Dillaway. Well, we're off. I'm here to get you up to Ghuru Nor just as fast as we can go. No delaying, or the line to Kalgan may be cut. Old man Holtz will take us out from Kalgan."

The Captain blinked his pale gray eyes and continued to watch Miss Dillaway.

"Gilbreth was worried about you," he said. "The Prince received him and is interested. His Highness is an educated man. I was going down here at any rate on business for the Prince—purchases—firearms. Gilbreth is twenty miles away from the palace, digging in a hill—funny business, digging."

"The palace," said Miss Dillaway. "Is there a palace?"

"You'll see it," the Captain answered. "A real palace with white and orange yurts in front and courtyards and red and yellow lama priests and attendants with peacock plumes. You can paint some pretty pictures there. Yes, it's quite a palace, like the days of Ghengis Khan."

Captain Hamby paused again, but it seemed to Calvin that his nasal unmusical voice still echoed above the rumbling of the train. He was not showing off now that he had spoken about himself. He had spoken and something of his past was with them on the train, turbulent and restive. Hearing, one could not help but wonder what had brought him there, but there was no doubt that everything he said was true.

"Don't blame you, if you don't believe me," Captain

78

Hamby said. "When you see the antelope and the camels and the prayer flags blowing and the black men with their pigtails and their pointed boots, I'll guarantee you'll think you're dreaming. It hasn't changed since Marco Polo except the Prince has a radio and guns."

"What does he want them for?" Calvin asked.

The Captain laughed shortly.

"You don't know the Asiatic situation," he said, "or else you'd know that Ghuru Nor is an important place right now. Mongolia's made up of principalities, and each prince is an independent little monarch. In the old days they dined once a year at table with the Emperor in Peking. The principality of Ghuru Nor has the old caravan route going through it, the shortest way to outer Mongolia and Russia, and the hills at Ghuru Nor are strategic. Either Russia or Japan wants them in case there is a war. I'll show you on the map tomorrow, except maps aren't worth much in Mongolia."

Miss Dillaway sat listening.

"Don't ask the Captain questions, Gates," she said. "I've never been there, Captain Hamby, but I guess it's about the same as any other place that's off the map. I've been in Persia and Mesopotamia and Central Africa. Is there typhus?"

"Yes," said Captain Hamby, "sometimes, Miss Dillaway."

"How's the water? Is there dysentery?"

"The water isn't bad," Captain Hamby said. "Not enough people to spoil it."

Miss Dillaway rose. "Well," she said, "I'm glad to hear it. I think I'll go to sleep. I'll see you in the morning, Captain."

Captain Hamby bowed.

"I knew you were all right just as soon as I saw you, Miss Dillaway," he said. "I guess I won't need to tell you anything, you know the ropes."

"Thanks," said Miss Dillaway. "I won't be any trouble."

The Captain sat down again when Miss Dillaway was gone and reached for the bottle.

"What a girl," he said. "What a girl."

79

"Yes," said Calvin Gates, "Miss Dillaway is very nice."

"That isn't what I meant," the Captain answered. "I meant she know her way around. I meant she hasn't got any silly ideas, and what's more she's beautiful." Captain Hamby sighed and took a sip of his whisky. "Yes, beautiful, and no wrong ideas."

Calvin Gates did not answer.

Captain Hamby disappeared through the narrow communicating door into his own compartment and came back in his shirt sleeves.

"What's the use of worrying," he was humming, "it never was worth while. How about another drink?"

"I don't mind," said Calvin Gates. Captain Hamby jerked his thumb toward the rear of the train.

"Everything all right back there?"

"Where?" asked Calvin Gates.

"Manchukuo. Were the Japanese all right? No trouble with the police?" The Captain's voice became lower and more confidential. "Nothing you want to tell me? Nothing on your mind?"

Calvin Gates put his hands in his pockets.

"No," he answered. "Why should there be?"

The Captain's gray eyes watched him steadily.

"No reason," he said, "except the Japanese are pretty officious these days. They're crawling around like flies at Ghuru Nor, dropping in all the time. Funny little fellows, nervous, always nervous."

"Yes," said Calvin Gates, "they're nervous."

The Captain jerked his thumb toward the rear of the train again.

"You're sure everything was all right back there?"

"Yes," said Calvin, "everything was perfectly all right."

"That's fine," the Captain said, "that's fine. You look pretty fit, Gates—as though you could take care of yourself. Be sure to lock your door to the passage and I'll leave the one between us open. You're sure there's nothing you want to tell me?"

They looked at each other for a moment in silence; Captain Hamby smiled invitingly.

"Only to thank you for the whisky," Calvin said.

"That's fine." Captain Hamby's smile grew broader.

"That's the way it ought to be. Just keep your door locked, Gates."

When he was alone Calvin realized that he was as tired as a swimmer who had been battered by waves into an acquiescent sort of weariness. His thin freckled face showed the strain of the last twenty-four hours, but the strain was more than physical. First there had been Mr. Moto and now there was Captain Hamby, both appearing out of nowhere. Logical as the explanation may have been, he knew that Captain Hamby was not there only to help Miss Dillaway. The Captain was made for more important tasks, and there was no mistaking those last remarks.

It was strange to think that Captain Hamby was just the sort of man he should have liked and that he represented all the things that Calvin Gates had wished to be, and yet, in spite of it, Calvin did not like him. Hamby had been a soldier for he had the stamp of the profession, which could never be described or entirely concealed. He had seen the world and had lived on danger and on change. Was he going on the same road as Captain Hamby, Calvin wondered?

The train swayed from side to side on the rough roadbed and the dark outside was like a door that shut him into his compartment while he was moving all the time farther from anything he knew. The compartment was a garish little place in the dim yellow electric light, without beauty or elaboration or extra comfort. The door leading to the Captain's sleeping place was closed. He pulled open his door to the passage and peered out into a dim smoky emptiness. When he closed the door again he found that there was no way to fasten it except by a sort of flat brass hook. He put the hook down carefully, glanced at Captain Hamby's closed door, and thrust his hand into the inside pocket of his coat. His fingers touched the cigarette case and he brought it out and laid it on his knee.

As far as he could see there was nothing extraordinary, either in its appearance or manufacture, that differed from dozens he had seen in jewelers' windows in Toyko. The work upon it, though delicate and beautiful, was not unusual in a land where minute skilled workmanship cost almost nothing. The silver had been cut straight through and black metal had been inlaid so that the design appeared both inside and outside the cover in a delicate silhouette. The result was a scene, familiar enough in Japanese and Chinese art, of small birds which rested, walked and flew among tufts of tall grasses, both black and delicate against the silver. He could see nothing more significant, look as he might inside and out, no sign of marks or scratching, and the metal was absolutely solid. The design was all that could mean anything. He remembered Mr. Moto's interest in the number of the birds, and now he counted six of them, three of them in the air, two perched upon the grasses, and one upon the ground.

He put the case back and reached into the side pocket of his coat. It was a thirty-eight caliber automatic which had been given him, of American make. He took out the clip and found that it was fully loaded, a dangerous thing to be carrying about in a land where he was a stranger. He finally took off his coat and rolled it up carefully, lay down on his berth and put the coat beneath his head. Then he switched off the light. The empty glasses on the little table rattled with the swaying of the car. The last thing he remembered was the rattling of the glasses.

It was also the first sound which came to his consciousness when he woke up, but he knew that such a harmless sound had not wakened him. He lay for a moment listening and then he slipped softly from his berth. The faint dusky light which filtered from the corridor outside showed him the compartment was empty. The train swayed and the glasses rattled and then there was another sound which came from the passageway outside—a dull metallic click. Someone was working quietly and expertly upon the lock of his door. Someone outside had thrust a knife blade through the crack and was lifting the brass catch, probably a simple enough matter for anyone who knew his business. His coat was still lying on the berth, and for a moment he thought of reaching for it before common sense stopped him and told him that the noise of a shot would arouse every passenger in the train. He stood hesitating, and then it was too late. The door was slid open gently, and the light in the passage revealed a squat, stocky figure which stood poised in the doorway for an instant. Then the figure moved and Calvin Gates moved also. The head of the intruder was turned away from him toward the empty berth when Calvin threw himself forward and landed square on the intruder's back. The impact threw the other off his balance and they both fell crashing against the table. At the same instant the man beneath him turned and Calvin could hear the sharp intake of his breath. A hand pulled at his collar and he saw that someone had turned on the light.

"Steady," he heard a voice saying, "steady." Someone was pulling at his shoulders and Calvin scrambled to his feet. His mind worked slowly and his ears were ringing. For a moment the whole place was hazy and then he saw a figure half sprawled across his berth. A hand was on his shoulder, shaking him, and it was Captain Hamby speaking.

"Steady," Captain Hamby said. "It's right as rain."

CHAPTER 11

CALVIN GATES spoke with difficulty and his voice sounded like a stranger speaking.

"I must have struck my head," he said.

"Steady," said Captain Hamby. "You'll be better in a minute."

"Someone came in here," said Calvin Gates.

"Yes," said Captain Hamby, "somebody came in. I hit him when you grabbed him. Everything's all right."

Calvin Gates shook his head and the haze was lifting, leaving the whole scene clear. A stocky, heavy man in cheap dark clothes lay sprawled half upon the floor and half upon the berth. His face was like a yellowish stupid mask with the lips and eyes half open. It was a brutal, ugly face and suddenly Calvin remembered. It was the man who had stepped through his hotel window at Mukden. Captain Hamby in his shirt sleeves was bending over holding a short riding crop. Calvin Gates looked behind him; the door to the passageway was closed.

"Pack up your troubles in your old kit bag," Captain Hamby was humming. "Smile boys, that's the style."

"You say you hit him?" Calvin asked.

Captain Hamby looked around with no emotion in his pale gray eyes and held up his riding crop.

"Hit him with three pounds of lead." he said. "Didn't know you were awake until you grabbed him. Handsome-looking johnny, ain't he? *Ronin.*"

"What?" said Calvin Gates.

"*Ronin.*" Hamby's gray eyes studied him impersonally. "That means strong-arm Japanese—the gunman type. Ugly-looking fellow, what?"

"Is he dead?" asked Calvin Gates.

"No," said Captain Hamby, "not quite. I hit him hard enough. Ugly fellow, isn't he? Not a nice chap to be dropping in at night." Captain Hamby laid his crop on the berth and rubbed his hands.

"Help me open the window, Gates."

"What for?" Calvin asked.

Captain Hamby's red face wrinkled into a grin.

"Because we don't want trouble," he said. "You follow me, don't you, Gates?"

"But you can't do that," Calvin Gates began, and Captain Hamby stopped smiling.

"Stow it, Gates," he said. "You know what he came in here for. It was either him or you, Gates. Maybe you didn't notice this. Look down there on the floor."

Calvin Gates looked down. A pistol with a silencer was lying at his feet.

"You see," said Captain Hamby, "it was either him or you. It don't pay to be fussy sometimes, Gates. Open the window. You take his head, I'll take his feet."

Calvin Gates opened the window. His mouth felt dry and his hands were shaking.

"While you've a lucifer to light your fag," Captain Hamby hummed, "smile boys, that's the style. Keep smiling. Heave him, Gates."

Captain Hamby turned away from the window and rubbed his hands.

"Well," he said, "nothing more to think about. Feeling all right, Gates?"

"Yes," said Calvin, "better, thank you."

"That's fine," said Captain Hamby, "fine. You didn't do so badly either. But you take my advice. Don't you try to wrestle with 'em. Hit 'em on the head." The Captain put his own head to one side and smiled.

"Anything you want to tell me, Gates?"

It was more of a request than a question, and Calvin Gates was puzzled. He still did not like the Captain, even when he had every reason to be grateful. The Captain's cool gray eyes stared at him and beyond him without warmth or interest, and they left Calvin Gates under no illusions that he would have been the one to go out the window if it had suited Captain Hamby.

Calvin reached for his coat where it lay on the berth and put it on and put his hand in his pocket.

"Hamby," he said, "I'm going to ask you something. Just where do you fit in?"

Captain Hamby picked up his riding crop and balanced it in his hand.

"Now we're talking sense," he said. "White men ought to stick together in this country, and we're going to stick together. You've been looking at me sideways, haven't you? I don't mind telling you I came down here to meet a Russian whose first name was Boris, who was acting as a guide for a lady name Miss Dillaway. Boris was planning to hand me a little personal favor in the shape of a silver cigarette case. What happened to Boris, Gates?"

"He's dead," said Calvin Gates.

Captain Hamby played absent-mindedly with his riding crop.

"I guessed it," he said. "The Japs popped him off, I suppose. I guessed it when I didn't see him. It couldn't be—excuse me if I seem impertinent—it couldn't be that he gave you a silver cigarette case, Gates? That couldn't be why you had a caller tonight?"

Calvin Gates nodded without speaking.

"That's fine," said Captain Hamby, "fine. So the Japs are on your trail, eh? And you and I are in the same boat. That's fine. I guess we better have a little talk."

Captain Hamby seated himself on the edge of the berth and rested his riding crop across his knees while his short, stubby fingers caressed it abstractedly.

"I don't like to be impertinent," Captain Hamby continued. "I've learned tolerance from the Chinese, Gates. They are the most civilized, tolerant people in the world. Anything goes within limits. The last thing I am is nosy; but I answered your question, now you answer one. Where do you fit in?"

It would have been a reasonable question—if there had not been a sort of personal offense in the Captain's voice which was a challenge to his instinct. He experienced an unreasoning antipathy for the cold-blooded self-assurance of that compact red-faced man, and at the same time something warned him to be careful—that Captain Hamby would use him so far only as he might be useful. Suddenly, Calvin knew that it was not accident but the deliberate action of part of his nature which had led him where he was. There was no use fooling himself. He had been happy in those ugly hours back in Mukden, and he was almost happy now. In spite of the blow on his head his mind was working smoothly.

"All right," he said, "I'll tell you. It takes a while to tell."

"That's fine." said Captain Hamby, "fine. Sit down, Gates. Let's talk like pals."

Calvin Gates sat down beside the Captain with his hand still in his coat pocket.

"It's this way," he began. "That Russian who was with Miss Dillaway on the boat—I didn't know either of them then—and then there was a Japanese named Mr. Moto—"

It seemed to him that the wrinkles about the Captain's eyes grew deeper and that his whole expression grew more intent.

"You know him?" Calvin asked.

"Brother," said Captain Hamby, "I know everybody. And Boris saw him, did he? Go ahead."

Calvin went on, drawing on a concise and accurate memory. He told of Mukden; he left out almost nothing, except the incident of the automatic pistol. Captain

Hamby fingered the riding crop across his knees and listened without comment. He listened as though the whole story were natural.

"What the use of worrying," he hummed softly, "it never was worth while ... That was fine work, fine. So you have the cigarette case, Gates?"

"Yes," said Calvin Gates.

"That's fine," said Captain Hamby. "Now you can hand it over."

Calvin sat up straighter. There was no mistaking Captain Hamby's urgency and eagerness. A light in Captain Hamby's gray eyes sent a quiver up Calvin's spine. Captain Hamby had no further use for him. Once Captain Hamby had the cigarette case Calvin knew that he would never get to Ghuru Nor. He would be disposed of like an empty bottle. The cigarette case had become a passport, as long as he kept it in his pocket.

"Not just yet," Calvin said.

Captain Hamby's expression was quizzical; he shifted his feet and coughed.

"Just why not, Gates?" he asked.

"Because I don't like the way you look," Calvin answered. "I'm not going to be tossed out that window too. You can have that case when you get us safely up to Ghuru Nor."

The Captain leaned a trifle farther forward. "Is that a fact?" he began, and then he stopped, dead still. Calvin Gates had pulled the pistol from his pocket. Captain Hamby raised his eyebrows and gazed at it thoughtfully.

"While you've a lucifer to light your fag," he hummed, "smile, boys, that's the style ... No reason for getting jumpy, Gates; my word, no reason at all. I was going to take you up to Ghuru Nor at any rate. There'll be fewer questions asked. Hand me over the case. I can keep it better—really."

"You'll get it when we get there," said Calvin Gates.

Captain Hamby shrugged his shoulders.

"Don't trust me, do you, Gates?" he asked.

"I trust you as long as I've got that case in my pocket," said Calvin Gates.

Captain Hamby's face wrinkled into a smile. "All right," he said, "all right. No hard feeling, Gates."

"No," said Calvin, "none at all."

"Mind you do what I tell you then," the Captain said. "We've got to travel quick."

"That's all right," said Calvin.

"That's fine," Captain Hamby said, "fine."

"Anything else you want to tell me?" asked Calvin Gates.

"No," said Captain Hamby, "nothing else, I think."

"Then perhaps you'll go where you belong," said Calvin Gates, "and if you'll excuse me I'm going to lock my door."

Captain Hamby rose from his seat on the edge of the berth, and Calvin followed his example.

"What's the use of worrying," Captain Hamby hummed. "No need to be jumpy, old man. I'll take care of you, never fear."

"I'm sure you will," Calvin answered.

"We'll get on fine when we understand each other." The Captain's tone was palcating and smooth. "So put away the sidearm, Gates, and how about shaking hands on it? We'll have to be pals, you know."

Captain Hamby held out his right hand. The gesture and his whole manner were suddenly disarming, but there was an involuntary contraction about the corners of his mouth. The shadow passed over the Captain's face and was gone, but Calvin Gates understood the expression as clearly as though the man had spoken. Calvin transferred his pistol from his right hand to his left and dropped it into his jacket pocket, but he did not take his hand away.

"Delighted to shake hands," he said.

The Captain's lips twitched slightly and then curved into his smile.

"No hard feeling, Gates," he said again. "We can take things as they come, can't we?"

"Absolutely," Calvin said.

"Fine," the Captain said. "We'll have a nice talk later on." There was no doubt that they understood each other. The Captain's manner had been almost perfect, but not quite. Calvin knew as sure as fate that the Captain had proposed to do something more than simply to shake his hand.

CHAPTER 12

AT HALF-PAST EIGHT the next morning Miss Dillaway knocked on his compartment door. She looked cheerfully neat and efficient. Outside the sun shone hot and brilliant out of a cloudless sky upon an unchanging landscape of mud villages and green fields. He could hear Captain Hamby moving about in his own quarters.

"While you've a lucifer to light your fag," Captain Hamby was singing, "smile, smile, smile."

Miss Dillaway was looking at him curiously.

"You don't seem very glad to see me," Miss Dillaway said. "What are you scowling at, Gates?"

"Smile, smile, smile," Calvin answered. "That song's getting on my nerves."

"Oh that's it, is it?" said Miss Dillaway. "It wouldn't hurt you to be like Captain Hamby. At any rate, he smiles."

The side of Calvin's head throbbed with a dull, constant pain, and that last remark of hers did not ease it. He felt that same unreasoning jealousy which he had experienced the night before. It seemed to him that she was through with him already.

"I wish we'd never laid eyes on him," Calvin said.

"You're being awfully silly, Gates," Miss Dillaway replied. "Why are you so rude to Captain Hamby?"

"What's so wonderful about him?" Calvin asked. "Do you like him because he sings?"

"Why Gates," said Miss Dillaway, "I don't particularly like him."

"Then why do you have to be so nice to him?" Calvin asked.

"Why, Gates," said Miss Dillaway, "why shouldn't we both be nice to him? He's helping us, isn't he?" There was a loud knock on the compartment door. It was Captain Hamby with his red face smooth and shining.

"Well, well," he said, "I'm not intruding, am I? I heard you talking. We'll be at Peiping inside an hour, right outside the walls. Sorry we have to go right through it, but we ought to connect with the train north with luck."

"What?" said Miss Dillaway, "aren't we going to stop?"

"Too bad, isn't it?" Captain Hamby smiled at her. "We better get north, I think. My job is to get you north." Miss Dillaway smiled back.

"Anything you say," she said, "but I'm sorry not to see Peiping."

"Don't you worry," Captain Hamby said, "you and I will see it some other time. Who wants a spot of breakfast?"

"I've had mine, thanks," Miss Dillaway said.

"Well, I haven't. Come on, Gates." Captain Hamby slapped Calvin on the shoulder. "You'll do better with some coffee, what?"

They walked together to a greasy dining car full of cigarette smoke.

"Too bad we have to hurry through," Captain Hamby said. His glance moved about the dining car as though he could see everything at once. "No need of telling Miss Dillaway about last night and no need to be so jumpy, Gates. You've figured me out wrong."

"I'm sorry if I did," Calvin said.

"Well, all I want is to have things smooth," said Captain Hamby. "Perhaps I was a bit put out last night, just a bit. We all have feelings, don't we, Gates? Yes, I was put out, but when I came to think it over I saw that you were right. It only means we're partners, don't it, Gates? So I'm going to lay the cards right down. Frank and open, that's my way. I'm nothing but an open book." The Captain's hard mouth creased into an ingratiating smile and he lighted a cigarette and allowed it to droop from his lower lip.

"It takes a bit of doing here to get along," he said. "I have a certain reputation, Gates. A lot of people when they want a job done think of Sam Hamby to do it. There'll be a spot of cash in this for you, Gates, if we deliver that cigarette case to the proper party. Three thousand dollars gold, not mex. I want you on our side."

Calvin Gates looked thoughtfully across the table.

That's quite a lot of money," he said.

"And all for you," said Captain Hamby. "I want you on our side."

Captain Hamby's eyes narrowed and he exhaled a puff of cigarette smoke from the corner of his mouth.

"Out in this country the way things are today anything can happen, anything does happen. If a pink elephant walked in here now I wouldn't turn a hair. I would only say it's China. Great place for a fellow to get along these days, if the fellow has the guts. Opium smuggling, gun running, bribery, war lords, bandits, spies—they're all outside the window there. The sky's the limit these days."

"I begin to think you're right," Calvin Gates agreed.

"Righto," said Captain Hamby cordially.

He could not understand what Captain Hamby was talking about, but he listened as though he understood.

"Facts," Captain Hamby said, "I like facts—and you and I know 'em, I guess. Here's China. Up there is Russia. Down there is Japan. Japan isn't through with China. She started on China and she can't stop now. Her Government is committed to dominate China and we know she's ready for another move. There's only one thing that makes her wait."

"Russia?" Calvin asked him.

"Righto," said Captain Hamby. "Russia doesn't want it. You know that, but here's something you don't know. Russia's got an army now. Let Japan start and Russia is going to strike her in the side and it won't be on the Amur River either. My word, Gates, she's going to move into Mongolia, and the first position she will occupy will be the hills at Ghuru Nor. My word, no fooling, she's ready to do it, Gates."

. "How do you know?" Calvin asked, but he was sure that Captain Hamby possessed some way of knowing. Hamby rubbed the side of his nose and smiled.

"No harm telling you," he said, "as long as you and I are traveling together, Ghuru Nor is only a day's march from Outer Mongolia, and that's the same as Russia. Russia will take that line of hills at Ghuru Nor and the road is clear to Kalgan. I know they're ready for it, because the Prince has been paid to let 'em in. The main thing is to get there before the Japs move in first. Do you get the picture now? Two divisions are up there waiting just one day's march off—waiting for the proper information. Well, there's where we come in."

"Where?" Calvin asked him, although he half knew where.

"No harm telling you," said Captain Hamby. "The Russian Intelligence is sending the message up to Ghuru Nor. It looks like the Japanese caught on, don't it? Cipher can be decoded. They were using another system. Well, they got Boris good and proper. It was a spot of luck he lighted onto you. Anything you want to say?"

Calvin Gates was silent for a moment, but he understood about the cigarette case now.

"If you looked at that cigarette case," he inquired, "could you tell what it meant? It's nothing but an ordinary commercial article."

Captain Hamby's reply was prompt and frank.

"No," he said, "I couldn't; but my word, they can read it where it's going. They'll be waiting for it at Kalgan."

Captain Hamby's glance darted about the dining car and rested on Calvin Gates. His face was cordial, but his glance was cool and distant.

"Surprises me that you don't ask something else," he said. "This Japanese johnny, Mr. Moto, where does he fit in? The police want one thing, and Mr. Moto wants something else. What about Mr. Moto, Gates? I need to find that out."

"I don't understand him," Calvin agreed; "not any more than you."

Captain Hamby's expression, though still agreeable, was less reassuring. He put another lump of sugar in his coffee and stirred it delicately; at the same time he began to hum a snatch of that refrain which seemed to have grafted itself like a disease upon his mind.

"Smile, smile, smile. . . . I don't like that coming from you after I've been on the up and up. You can't think I'm so wooly in the head that I don't know that Moto is one

92

of the tidiest secret agents in Japan. I've seen Moto in Nanking and I've seen him in Shanghai, and wherever that little blighter goes, trouble comes right after him. Are you going to tell me about Mr. Moto, Gates?"

The Captain's expression was mocking but restrained. What this implied was so unexpected that Calvin Gates found it difficult to answer.

"Look here," he said, "I don't know what you're driving at. I'm going up to join the Gilbreth Expedition at Ghuru Nor. I've told you everything I know about Mr. Moto."

"Oh my," said Captain Hamby. "So you don't want to talk, eh? I'm giving you an out, Gates. I'm making you a proposition, don't you see?"

"No," said Calvin Gates, "I don't see"—and it was true. He had never been as completely nonplussed as he was when he studied Captain Hamby's face across the table.

"My word, it don't do any good to bluff," Captain Hamby said, and his voice was placating again. "We're white men, Gates, and we're the same sort of white men, looking out where our bread is buttered, aren't we? My word, you had me puzzled for a while when I saw you there in Shan-hai-kuan. That confused look on your face, it was all done so neat and tidy. My word, it was, until you spoke of Mr. Moto. And then I saw the gun—tourists don't carry guns." Captain Hamby spoke more softly and tapped his blunt forefinger on the table emphasizing every word. "Moto gave you that case. You're carrying it for him. It's time to sell out, Gates, or else you can let me in. What does Moto want? Are the Japs moving in to Ghuru Nor?"

The deliberate, unmusical tones of Captain Hamby's voice struck into Calvin's ears with an umpleasant physical sensation. At last he could understand completely what Captain Hamby meant. He might talk himself blue in the face and Hamby would not believe him. There was nothing for him to do but accept the situation.

"I don't know what Mr. Moto wants," he said.

"My word, fellow," said Captain Hamby, "don't you see your number's up? Come now, I don't know your his-

93

tory. Was it the army? I was cashiered myself. Or maybe it was larceny that got you here, taking somebody's money, what? When the Japanese get their hands on a white man it's always something like that. Tell it to your uncle, Gates. Some jam, eh what, and Mr. Moto comes along?"

"I don't know what he wants," said Calvin Gates. The dining room suddenly seemed insufferably hot. He pulled out a handkerchief and mopped his forehead.

"Got the wind up, have you, Gates?" Captain Hamby said. "Guessed it right, didn't I? Come now, what's Moto to you? I'm offering you three thousand gold to tell me what he wants."

Calvin Gates put his handkerchief back in his pocket. "I told you I don't know what he wants," he said.

Captain Hamby's lips pressed themselves tight together; his gray eyes had never looked colder.

"So that's the way it lies, is it, Gates? You won't play in with me?"

"I'll paddle my own canoe, thanks," said Calvin Gates.

"Oh!" Captain Hamby's face was ugly. "I'm not offering enough money, am I, Gates?"

Captain Hamby rested his chin on the palm of his hand, and the wrinkles deepened about the corners of his eyes.

"I don't make it out," he said. "You certainly have guts, Gates. I wonder if you know how much. It don't pay to run afoul of me, not ever. You're going to get what's coming to you just as sure as fate."

"Thanks for telling me," Calvin said. Captain Hamby pushed back his chair.

"Yes," he said, "you've got guts. We know where we stand, don't we, Gates? I hope you know what you're doing. We better go back and get off the train. What's the use of worrying, it never was worth while."

Captain Hamby walked out of the car in front of him, still humming his favorite tune.

"While you've a lucifer to light your fag," Captain Hamby was humming, "smile, boys, that's the style."

But Calvin knew that Captain Hamby was not smiling. He could not forget Captain Hamby's look as he had arisen from the table. The fact had been as hard and as competent as ever, but somehow it had been marked by indecision. The day was sweltering hot but Calvin Gates felt cold.

Miss Dillaway was in her compartment closing her bag.

"Here," said Captain Hamby, "let me lend a hand, Miss Dillaway."

Miss Dillaway smiled at him and it seemed to Calvin Gates that there was no reason to be so civil. He walked to his own compartment and sat there waiting. He still could not recover from his surprise at what Captain Hamby thought of him. Mr. Moto knew of him as a fugitive from justice and Captain Hamby considered him an employee of Japan.

"I must tell Dillaway," he murmured to himself. "Dillaway will think that's funny."

He sat by the window trying to think. Outside he could see a long gray city wall and he did not need to be told what wall it was. The train had reached Peiping.

The guidebook had told Calvin Gates a few facts, but it had been his experience that facts very seldom conveyed much useful information. The guidebook had informed him that the Peiping-Mukden line on which they were traveling arrived at the Chien Men East Station which lay inside the Chinese City and just south of the Tartar City Wall. Kalgan, where they were going, was reached by a different railroad, the Peiping-Suiyuan line, and it would be necessary to travel across the city to make the connection. He did not know the dramatic intricacies of the city of Peiping, where walls and gates divided the whole area into quarters like armed camps and where the houses themselves and parts of houses stood behind more walls, making Peiping the most private, remote and mysterious city in the world. He had not even heard, or if he had he could not understand the significance, of the Chinese City, the Tartar City, the Imperial City, and finally the Forbidden City in the center of it all, a vacant shell where the yellow tiled roofs, the pavilions and palaces of a dead empire shone behind high pink stuccoed walls.

The fact conveyed nothing until he got off the train, and then he saw the massive wall of slate-colored brick, a huge curtain of defense towering above the train shed—a last remnant of the barbaric magnificence of Peiping, when it had been the center of the greatest empire in the world.

He stood with his trench coat over his arm momentarily forgotten by everyone while the Chinese porters, their breaths heavy with garlic and their shaven heads and faces dripping with perspiration, piled the baggage out of the car and strapped it across their shoulders. Captain Hamby must have sent word ahead, because it was evident that they had been expected. A tall gaunt Chinese in a black silk robe had come running on slippered feet to the Captain the moment they were off the train, and Captain Hamby had moved a yard or so away with him, and now the Captain was talking volubly and earnestly in Chinese, occasionally moving his hand in a quick gesture. Calvin knew that he and Miss Dillaway formed a part of the conversation, for he saw that black solemn man glance towards them once or twice.

Again Calvin Gates had a helpless feeling. The startling brilliance of the sun, the round, well-fed faces of the khaki-clad Chinese police, the blue and black Chinese gowns, the chatter of the porters and hotel runners while the passengers descended in a steady stream and moved toward the station gate—all had a menacing aspect.

Those strange sights and the aching of his head and the bright sunlight must have made him stupid, for he did not realize that anything was wrong until Captain Hamby had left him standing on the station platform with Miss Dillaway. Then he saw that something had upset her. She had been happy enough that morning, but now her face was pale and drawn.

"Gates," she began, and stopped, and her voice as much as her face startled him. She was looking at him strangely, no longer as a friend might look, but curiously and with a sort of compassion. Something surely had happened in those last minutes on the train, but he could think of nothing which had been unusual.

"Dillaway," he said, "what is it?" And he took her by the arm, but she wrenched her arm away.

"Look here," said Calvin Gates. "What is it?"

96

"Don't touch me," she said. "Don't you ever dare to touch me. Captain Hamby's told me, Gates."

"What did he tell you?" Calvin stammered. "Look here, Dillaway, what's the matter?"

"Do you mean to stand here and ask me that?" Her voice was low and vibrant. "After what you've done?"

All he could do was to stare at her in blank amazement. Her attack had been so sudden, and he had thought that they were friends. His surprise was changing into a sort of desperation. Now that it had gone so mysteriously, he valued that friendship.

"Dillaway," he stammered, "I haven't done anything to you. I hope to die if I've ever——"

She interrupted him in a low, choked voice.

"It makes me so ashamed," she said, "ashamed that I ever spoke to you. You haven't done anything? My God, Gates, but I've been an idiot about you! Captain Hamby's told me. Now do you understand?"

His own expression must have frightened her, because she drew back from him.

"Hamby?" Calvin said. "So he was talking to you when he fixed your bag, was he? Well, what did he say? I don't understand."

"Don't," said Miss Dillaway sharply. "That only makes it worse." And her voice trembled. "God knows why I'm giving you a chance. I suppose because I liked you. I suppose I should have known it myself, after seeing you with that Japanese at the hotel and after seeing you drinking tea with that other Japanese at the station. There isn't any doubt about it, Gates. It only makes it worse if you try to lie. You've used me as something to hide behind. You're working for the Japanese, Gates, and Captain Hamby knows it."

Her words were as dazzlingly blinding as the sunlight.

"Dillaway——" said Calvin Gates, and he found that he was pleading with her. He was pleading and struggling against that suspicion in her mind because it was taking her away from him, and yet he could see the logic of the suspicion. He was struggling with fantastic shadows.

"Dillaway," he pleaded. "Won't you please listen, Dillaway? Don't look at me like that. Don't you know me well enough to know that I couldn't be mixed up in such a thing? I told you about Mr. Moto, Dillaway. I care about your good opinion more than anything. I'd rather die than have you think that I'd made use of you."

Miss Dillaway shook her head.

"I'm giving you your chance, Gates," she said. "You'd better give me that cigarette case and get away while you can. I'm not blaming you, but it's sort of a surprise. I thought I liked you, Gates."

An ugly look come over Calvin's face.

"Did Hamby suggest that?" he asked.

"No," she answered in that same tired voice. "I suggested it to him. I don't want you to be hurt, Gates."

Calvin felt his fingernails bite into the palms of his hands.

"That's kind of you," he said. "And you believe that black-leg and you don't believe me?"

"But what are you?" she answered. "Why should I believe you, Gates?"

He was calm again. Life had clamped upon him with an icy finality.

"Well," he said, "that's you. There's no reason why you should if you don't want to. You'd rather keep on with Captain Hamby than go along with me?"

"Dr. Gilbreth sent him," she said.

"All right," Calvin answered. "If you think Hamby's more honest than I am, go ahead, I'm through. Did he tell you whom he was working for? Probably not, because he's willing to work for anyone if he gets the money. I was going to make the best of his society on account of you. Lord knows what he'll do when he gets this, but here it is. Take your cigarette case and go along with Hamby, Dillaway. It may help you more than me right now—as long as you look at things this way." And he took the cigarette case from his pocket and put it in her hand. Miss Dillaway fumbled with her pocketbook, dropped the cigarette case inside it and closed it with a snap.

"Gates," she said, "I want you to know I'm not angry. I couldn't be angry with anyone like you, but I never want to see you again."

"Well," Calvin said, "that's plain enough." He turned

98

on his heel and the station platform was unsteady beneath his feet, and he did not turn to look back. He did not care even to stop for his baggage. He was through.

"Here," Hamby called to him. "Where are you going, Gates?"

He was able to answer carelessly.

"Just to the end of the platform," he said, "I'm just going to stretch my legs."

He was going to stretch his legs a good long way, but he strolled along carelessly because Hamby was watching him. He felt better with every step he took.

"Well," he said to himself, "that's that."

He surrendered his ticket at the gate and walked quickly through the station. He was through with it, just as he had said.

CHAPTER 13

HE REALIZED with a sense of shock how angry he had been only when he reached the sunlit square outside the station. The anger and the indignation which he felt had been like a touch of sun which had burned away his wits, leaving him standing pale and abstracted, like the survivor of some great disaster. Although she had sent him away, he knew that he should not have gone, but now everything they had both said seemed irreparable.

Then a single definite thought came into his mind. There had been another disaster which had brought him to that place. He must go ahead by himself to that other railroad station and take that other train. He had crossed the ocean to see a man named Dr. Gilbreth at a place called Ghuru Nor. Voices came to him through his thoughts, and brought his mind back to the present. Hands were twitching at his sleeves, and he saw that he stood before the station in the middle of a crowd of perspiring Chinese.

"Rickshaw," they were shouting at him, "rickshaw, marster?"

It was that insistent clamor that made him realize that he had no idea of where to go; but there was one person in the crowd who seemed to understand his desire. A large Chinese in a visor cap kicked his way through the ring of rickshaw coolies and touched Calvin's arm. His face was as round and benign as a harvest moon. He was wearing a shabby chauffeur's uniform.

"Taxicab," he said in a liquid, bell-like voice. "Nice taxicab. This way, marster."

"Yes," said Calvin.

"Quick all time," came the answer. "This way, marster."

Later Calvin remembered that he never said where he wished to go. Smilingly the driver pointed to a closed black automobile of an antiquated type.

"Nice car, marster," the Chinese said, "nice clean. Get in, marster," and he opened the door with one hand and supported Calvin's arm with the other.

Calvin's foot was on the running board, when a hand against his back sent him inside sprawling and the door of the car slammed shut. Something hard was prodded into Calvin's back.

"Get up on the sit," a voice said.

Still on his hands and knees, Calvin glanced sideways. The voice had told him already that a Japanese was speaking and there he was, a small man like the rest of his race, with a square jaw and a blunt nose. His dark eyes were narrow and ugly. He was jabbing a small blunt pistol repeatedly at Calvin's side, and he spoke slowly and distinctly.

"Get up on the sit. You come with me," he said.

Then Calvin understood what had happened; it was the cigarette case again, and they thought he had the case. He got up from his hands and knees and sat down and turned his head to look at his captor. There he was in shoddy European clothes like a million of his countrymen, and he evidently knew his business. He held the pistol close to Calvin's side.

"What are you going to do?" Calvin asked. It was a foolish question. The Japanese pushed his ribs with the pistol and spoke carefully with a pause between each word.

"You sit still," he said, "and shut up your damn mouth."

Calvin Gates leaned back and folded his hands across his knee with no further desire for conversation. Yet even in that stunned moment of his surprise he remembered thinking that the words with which he had been addressed were the first words of rudeness or insolence that he had heard from anyone of the Japanese or Chinese race. It was not a pleasant omen. It meant that he was as good as finished and no longer worth consideration. It would have been different if they had not thought that the cigarette case was in his pocket, and then he thought of something else. The same thing might happen to Miss Dillaway when they found it was not there. No matter what the provocation had been, he should not have left her. He moved uneasily and the pistol prodded back into his ribs.

His resentment and his pride disappeared when the pistol prodded into his ribs, but it was too late. Given the opportunity, his own strength was greater than that of the square-jawed man beside him; and the desire to use his strength almost overcame any prudence until the pressure on his side reminded him that he might as well have been tied hand and foot. He could see the thick neck of the Chinese chauffeur in the seat in front, and the car was already moving. It moved along a broad street past a pink stucco wall with yellow tiles on top. He had a glimpse of a moat with white marble bridges arching over it, and next they were threading their way through broad thoroughfares with blank gray walls and red doorways, past rickshaws whose occupants carried sunshades above their heads, past Chinese who stood on the corners cooling themselves with brightly colored fans, past old men carrying bird cages, past carts being drawn by sweating men. The ride was not a long one. The car finally swerved out of one of those broad streets into a narrow alley so suddenly that he was thrown against the man beside him. The Japanese struck him hard on the side of his face and jabbed the pistol into his ribs again.

"You sit still," he said.

101

Calvin spoke for the second time.

"I won't forget that," he answered, and the Japanese struck him again.

"You shut your mouth," he said.

They were in a narrow, unpaved alley with high blank walls on either side of it, and the car had stopped in front of a broad red gate. They waited only for the driver to blow his horn before the gate swung open, allowing them to drive into a broad courtyard where they stopped again. The Chinese driver, still bland and smiling, opened the car door.

"Get out. You follow him," his captor said.

They were in a large dusty enclosure bounded by high walls with long narrow buildings erected against them, the roofs of which shimmered from the heat of the sun. The courtyard was paved with gray mud brick, and had been swept scrupulously clean. The cleanliness was what he remembered best, and the fresh red paint on the doors and the latticed windows. Calvin knew that he was in the outer courtyard of a large establishment which might have been a native hostelry or perhaps a palace, and the walls shut him in as securely as the entrance to a prison, away from any sort of help and away from any possibility of escape. He felt the pistol in the small of his back, as he followed the Chinese driver. The sound of their feet as they clattered on the gray stone tiles made him wonder if he would ever walk back that way alive and the chances of doing so seemed slight. A weight in his right-hand jacket pocket reminded him that he was still armed. Apparently no one had given the possibility of his carrying a weapon serious attention. Even so it did not help with a pistol leveled at his back.

He followed obediently to one of the buildings by the wall, halting while the driver opened a door and stood aside. A further prod of the pistol on his back was his order to walk ahead.

Whatever was going to happen to him would happen soon, and the thought caused him no great fear. His only desire was not to die unless the man behind him died with him. He knew it was not a proper thought for such a time, but it stopped him from being afraid.

He stepped over a high threshold into a room which seemed dark after the glare outside, until his eyes became accustomed to the light. Then he saw that it was a large, long room, one side of which was a bare wall, and that light came through four windows which faced the courtyard, a soft light that filtered through rice paper, which was pasted over the windows in place of glass. It showed the bare beams of the building above him supported by a line of smooth red columns, and the beams were carved and colored in blues and reds and gold. At one end of the room was what he took for a platform covered with matting, with a small teakwood table upon it. The only other furnishing was a long bench against the wall. His guard walked in directly behind him and the driver closed the door leaving them alone. In the silence which followed Calvin could hear a pattering of feet and voices in the courtyard.

"Stand up," the Japanese said. "Stand still." And he pointed his pistol at Calvin's head. Calvin leaned against one of the pillars and shrugged his shoulders. The man in front of him grinned at him.

"Funny aren't you?" Calvin said. There was no response, but the pistol was still pointed at his head.

He realized that it was meant to be amusing, and that he was not to be shot just yet. They were obviously waiting for someone and they did not have to wait long. It could not have been more than a minute before the door opened again, making a rectangle of bright sunlight, and a man in clean white linen stepped over the high threshold and slammed the door shut.

Though it was still hard for him to distinguish the features of one Asiatic from another, he was certain that the newcomer was also Japanese in spite of his being larger than most of his race. He was a broad-shouldered, muscular man of middle age, and the first Japanese that Calvin had seen who looked entirely at home in European clothes. His figure might have been that of a European in the white suit, but in spite of the civilian clothes he was, like Captain Hamby, a military man, with the soldier's posture and the soldier's brisk, decisive step. When the light struck the side of one of his high cheeks Calvin saw two scars. He had seen the same on the cheeks of Prussian officers, the scars from a German students' duel. They were deep enough to have effected the muscles in one corner of the mouth, so that one corner drooped down slightly while the other tilted up.

The man in white gave a sharp order and Calvin's guard drew back, still holding his pistol ready. He halted in front of Calvin and stood with his hands clasped behind his back and spoke in a sharp, businesslike voice in English that was slurred by a German accent.

"You're an American named Calvin Gates," he said.

It occurred to Calvin that there was no reason to be polite.

"And I take you for a Japanese educated in Germany," he answered. "You know my name, but I don't know yours."

The mouth of the man turned upward one corner, but the other corner remained immobile.

"Quite right," he said. "You are speaking to Major Ahara of the Japanese army."

"That's interesting," said Calvin Gates, "but it doesn't mean a thing to me."

The corner of the Major's mouth twisted upward for a second time.

"I have never liked Americans," he said. "I hope very soon we go to war with America. It will be so after we finish our business here."

"That's interesting," said Calvin Gates.

The Major looked at him with frank distaste.

"I dislike Americans very much," he said, "so I do not care to talk. I am informed you have a cigarette case with you."

"What of it?" said Calvin Gates.

The Major unclasped his hands from behind his back.

"You will give it to me at once," he said.

Calvin Gates still leaned against the red pillar. The guard was listening, interested. He had lowered his pistol, but he still held it in his hand.

"And then what?" Calvin said.

The Major's lips twitched.

"You and I both know then what, Mr. Gates," he answered.

"Very well," said Calvin Gates. "There's no use lying to you." And he put his right hand into his jacket pocket. The Major took a step forward, holding out his hand.

"That is sensible of you," he said, "and if you answer questions freely you'll have an easier time. You will be made to talk at any rate."

"That's considerate of you, Major," Calvin said.

His hand had tightened over the pistol. It was out of his pocket and he fired at just the same instant. The single shot made a roaring sound. The guard had staggered backward against the wall. The Major was standing in front of him, and Calvin took a step backward.

"That wasn't so bright of you, Major," he said. "You Japanese are always so damn sure. Don't you ever search people when you catch them?"

The Major raised a hand to his head. He was no longer an army officer with a brisk military manner; his voice was quiet and subdued.

"Will you please to kill me now," he said. "The information was you were not armed. I wish you would kill me please before the rest come."

"Sensitive, aren't you?" said Calvin Gates. "Don't worry, you'll go when I go."

He paused a moment, listening. He could hear voices and footsteps in the courtyard and the sound of a motor horn, but no one came near the door. The man he had shot had sunk down to the bench, groaning softly and holding his hand against his side, but no one came near the door. Calvin grinned at the Major.

"It looks as though they thought that shot was meant for me," he said.

The Major's face twitched and he repeated his plea again.

"I wish you would kill me, please," he said.

Calvin Gates moved toward him.

"Proud, aren't you?" he said, and he shifted the pistol from his right hand to his left. "Kill yourself if you want to. I'd rather do it this way," and he struck the Major on the jaw. He saw the eyes glaze and the mouth fall open, and he struck again.

The Major was sinking to his knees and Calvin watched him. He had struck him twice with all his force, and the Major would be no trouble for a while.

Calvin Gates stood still and his face assumed an expression almost of stupid surprise as the consciousness of what he had done came over him. What amazed him most was that it had been so easy, and he had the same sort of astonishment that comes to an amateur at a gambling table after a series of successive winnings. In less than half a minute, for the first time in his life, he had fired upon a human being as coolly as though he were practising a snap shot in a shooting gallery. Instead of hitting an abstract mark he had hit a human being and had inflicted what was probably a fatal wound. A moment later he had beaten a second individual into temporary insensibility, and it all had occurred almost as fast as thought.

He had never realized his own capacity until just then, and it had an ironic significance. Standing there in that strange place, the conviction came upon him that he was doing exactly what he had always wanted, for he had always longed to be in danger. For once in his life he had achieved what he wanted, and now that he had achieved it he was not greatly elated, for he suddenly understood that his whole life had been built for such a situation and that he was only useful in such surroundings.

Now that he was faced with the reality, it was not much to be proud of, for the thing which he had done was out of keeping with his sense of fitness and humanity. Yet now that he had done it, there was no time for drawing back. He would have to go on very quickly, if he were to avail himself even of the slender chance of getting out of that courtyard and into the street alive.

Even while he was thinking, another part of him began to act. He found himself stepping toward the doorway with an even, unhurried step. At the same time he was thinking that he could do all this more easily again if he came out alive; he would be better equipped to kill and less appalled at facing the prospect. He would be like

Captain Hamby, given time; it was the only thing he was good for, to be like Captain Hamby.

He understood very clearly that he must open the door and walk out into the court. The casualness of his appearance might provoke a moment of uncertainly which might allow him time to reach the gate. If anyone attempted to stop him, he must shoot again without compunction, and he felt no great compunction; he was getting more like Hamby all the time.

The courtyard had been empty when he had crossed it, but now he could hear voices which were raised in some sort of altercation. Whatever might be happening outside, it was too late for him to stop. Putting his pistol back in his jacket pocket, but still holding his hand over it, Calvin opened the door and stepped out into the brilliant sunshine.

The instant that he was in the courtyard, however, the pistol was out again and ready in his hand, while the scene outside flashed accurately across his mind, at first with only the significance that comes to a marksman. Across the court standing by the door of another of those buildings built against the wall was a knot of Japanese. They had not even noticed his appearance, for all their attention was focused upon the center of the courtyard. The antiquated black car which had brought him still stood there empty, and beside it was a smaller, tan-colored vehicle with a driver in a khaki uniform at the wheel. Midway between that brown automobile and where he stood, three Japanese stood arguing excitedly. All these details flashed before him instantaneously, just as he stepped over the high Chinese threshold. The three in the center of the courtyard saw him at the same instant, and their voices stopped.

"Run," his mind was saying; "get over to the gate."

Then one of the three was walking toward him holding up his hand.

"Please," he was calling. "One moment, Mr. Gates." And Calvin recognized the voice, and the black-and-white golf suit and the golden smile. It was Mr. Moto, walking toward him blandly.

"So nice to see you, Mr. Gates," Mr. Motto spoke quickly. "So fortunate."

His speech ended in a quick sibilant hiss, and he assumed a queer fixed smile. "Will you please come with me now, or I am so afraid that we will both be killed?"

There was no doubt that it was Mr. Moto. His appearance in that checked suit was as preposterous as his words, but Mr. Moto took his clothes and his words entirely for granted.

"How did you get here?" Calvin asked him, still holding his pistol ready. Mr. Moto's reply was brisk and businesslike.

"No need for the pistol now, please," Mr. Moto said. "I came by airplane. I cannot understand. This is very terrible. They do not like me here. Army officers are so very, very cross. So many factions in Japan. Please follow me. Do not shoot unless I tell you."

In spite of the merry contour of his mouth, there was a nervous tremor in his fingers and his eyes blinked rapidly.

"You must not spoil everything," said Mr. Moto, "when I work so hard. I thought that I understood Americans. Sorry to be rude. Do not talk but follow me."

Mr. Moto spun quickly on his heel and began walking back toward the little brown car, and Calvin followed. The two Japanese stood near the automobile, wooden-faced, youngish men, both scowling sullenly.

"Get in," Mr. Moto said, and then he spoke volubly in Japanese. His words made a snapping sound like electric sparks. One of the young men snapped a sentence back and Mr. Moto drew a paper from his pocket and tapped it with his forefinger. Whatever was written upon it seemed conclusive, for without another word Mr. Moto also climbed into the car and gave an order to the driver. The engine started and the car rolled through the gate. Mr. Moto's breath whistled softly through his teeth.

"So glad," he said. "The army faction is so very hard to deal with. What happened please?"

"I shot a man," said Calvin Gates. He felt stupid and dull from the reaction. "They grabbed me at the station—I suppose it's that damned cigarette case."

108

He found himself staring at Mr. Moto, who nodded sympathetically.

"So sorry," Mr. Moto said. "Such a bad mistake for you to leave your friends. The military faction are so impetuous. Ha ha. Our soldiers are so brave, but so very, very rash. I came as soon as I had heard."

"You came from where?" said Calvin Gates.

"Please," said Mr. Moto, "it does not matter. We are going where it will be safer for us please. We will be like friends and have whisky like Americans. What happened please? I hope they were polite."

"They were going to kill me, and you know it," said Calvin Gates.

"Oh yes," said Mr. Moto, "they would liquidate, of course, but I hope so much that they were polite. I should not wish to report rudeness. What happened, please?"

Mr. Moto listened and rubbed his hands together, and looked troubled.

"That is very serious," he said, "that they should have been so impolite. It makes me very, very angry. There is no reason to be impolite in a liquidation. I have seen so many where everything was nice."

Mr. Moto smiled as though he had hit upon a happier thought.

"But you shot the man who struck you, did you not? So much nicer for your honor. And the major with the scar upon his cheek. That is Major Ahara. Ha ha. He has tried to kill me in the political troubles, but he is a very lovely man. He always loved his flowers. Such very beautiful azaleas in his garden, Mr. Gates. I heard the first shot, but I did not hear the second. I hope so very, very much you shot him also. . . . You did not? I cannot understand. Americans are so very, very puzzling. So much kinder to have killed him than have struck him, Mr. Gates. Excuse me—so much more polite. You are so very, very puzzling, Mr. Gates."

"Why?" asked Calvin Gates, and he felt that his wits were leaving him.

Mr. Moto sighed softly.

"Because I am so afraid that now he must kill himself. You understand that he is in too much disgrace. So lucky

109

for you that he did not search you, and so like some younger officers. It has to do with the more radical wing of our military party, Mr. Gates, and they are so much out of hand."

If most of what Mr. Moto had said was not entirely comprehensible, there was one thing of which Calvin was entirely convinced.

"I wish I had never set eyes on you," he said.

CHAPTER 14

MR. MOTO raised his hand before his mouth and drew in his breath.

"So sorry," he said, "but excuse me, Mr. Gates, this was all so unnecessary. I had made such careful plans. I had tried to think about you and just what you would do. There was a lady on the train, such a very lovely lady, and yet you did not stay with her. I do not understand. You would have been safe with Captain Hamby."

Calvin Gates was startled.

"How did you know about Hamby?" he asked.

"Please," said Mr. Moto, "it does not matter. All that matters is that I am so very stupid. I was so sure that you would stay with Captain Hamby and the lady. I do not see, indeed I do not see. But surely you gave Captain Hamby the cigarette case with the little birds upon it?"

Calvin Gates shook his head, and Mr. Moto gave a start, but his face was inscrutable. All the complicated repressions of a complicated race made it difficult to read.

"I didn't trust him," said Calvin Gates.

Mr. Moto's hands rubbed against each other nervously.

"So very silly of me," he said. "I had never thought of that. When I heard that Captain Hamby had come to meet you, I thought there would not be the slightest doubt. You are so very difficult, Mr. Gates. You leave the lady, and now you have the cigarette case with you. I had not thought of that."

"I haven't got it," Calvin told him.

He had not believed that Mr. Moto could display such emotion. Mr. Moto half rose from his seat and struck his hand on his forehead.

"Did they take it from you back there?" he almost shouted. "Quickly, Mr. Gates."

Mr. Moto's cheeks had grown greenish and sallow, and he seized Calvin by the lapel of his coat.

"No," said Calvin, "they didn't take it."

Mr. Moto groaned and muttered something in his own language.

"This is so very terrible," he groaned. "You did not throw it away?" and his fingers twitched at Calvin's coat lapel.

"No," Calvin said. "You needn't pull at me, Mr. Moto. I gave the thing back to Miss Dillaway. We had a quarrel and I got angry. I wish I'd never seen it or you, Mr. Moto. I'm worried about Miss Dillaway."

Mr. Moto sank back in his seat. The color had returned to his cheeks and he sighed deeply.

"Excuse my rudeness, please," he said. "I was so very startled. So Miss Dillaway has it then. But you spoke to Captain Hamby about that cigarette case? Surely you did that?"

Calvin moved his shoulders impatiently.

"Well," he said, "what's going to happen to her? I know that thing is dangerous for her, Moto. Of course I spoke to Hamby about it. He told me what it was—a code message going to the Russians. It's military information, and instead of trying to intercept it, you do everything to have it go through. Hamby knows about you, Moto, and he thinks I'm helping you. He offered me three thousand dollars if I would tell him what you wanted."

He had expected the news to be disturbing, but instead Moto gave a little jump in his seat and clapped his hands.

"Oh," said Mr. Moto, "that is so very nice. So exactly what I wished. I am so obliged to you, Mr. Gates. So very much obliged."

Calvin Gates scowled at him.

"What's going to happen to that message and what's going to happen to Miss Dillaway?" he asked. "Aren't you going to stop it?"

"Please," said Mr. Moto, "that is why I have worked so hard. I do not wish to stop it. It must not be disturbed. It is going to a man in Kalgan named Mr. Holtz, and now I think it will surely go there. It is so very nice."

"Moto," Calvin asked him, "are you a patriotic Japanese?"

Mr. Moto looked as though the question pained him.

"I should be so pleased to die for my emperor," he said. "This is all so very nice. You have done me such a service, Mr. Gates. The army will be angry at you, but I shall see that you are safe. So nice that Captain Hamby knows so much," and Mr. Moto smiled as though some secret joke of his own amused him.

"I've learned quite a lot on this train ride, Mr. Moto," Calvin said. "Do you know the Russians have two divisions they are going to move to this place called Ghuru Nor? Do you know that, and do you mean to say that you're not going to stop that message?"

Mr. Moto turned his head toward Calvin with a quick birdlike gesture and smiled and rubbed his hands.

"This does not concern you, Mr. Gates," he said. "Why are you so interested?"

"Because I want to know what's going to happen to Miss Dillaway," Calvin said. "She has that cigarette case."

"Then why did you not stay with her?" said Mr. Moto. "What was it that made you angry?"

Calvin scowled at the little man on the seat beside him and repressed a growing desire to shake him. His motives were entirely beyond him, but he could not help but admire Mr. Moto in a way.

"Hamby told her I was a Japanese spy," he said. "I've got a good deal to thank you for, Moto. He told her I was a Japanese spy, and she said I was making use of her."

Mr. Moto put his hand before his mouth and his shoulders began to shake.

"Excuse me," said Mr. Moto, "it is so rude to laugh. Things are so difficult, but they are so very funny. I have been using both of you I think. Ha ha, I am using everyone. And they caught you back there and they never

112

knew you had such information. So sorry if I laugh, Mr. Gates. You will laugh too when you understand."

Mr. Moto rubbed his hand across his eyes.

"I've found you," Mr. Moto said, "in the offices of the Intelligence section of the staff of our Third Army. You had the information of Russia they are trying so hard to get. Excuse me, your position is so confusing."

Calvin Gates scowled back at him.

"To hell with your nonsense, Moto," he said. "Miss Dillaway's got that cigarette case. What's going to happen to her?"

Mr. Moto's face became dull and masklike.

"I hope so much that nothing bad will happen," he said. "It depends on Captain Hamby, I am so afraid. You do not understand me very well, but I am so obliged to you, Mr. Gates. I think I shall not need you any further. We will talk about your plans in just a minute. We are going to the house of a friend of mine, a very important Japanese friend. He is not there, but you will be so very welcome. We are arriving now, I think."

Calvin Gates had not noticed where they had been going. He had lost all sense of direction long ago and nearly all sense of time. He was moving in a sort of fantasy not relieved by Mr. Moto's conversation and Captain Hamby's remark that anything might happen was growing increasingly true. The car had stopped in another alley which was almost like the one they had left, before another red gate in another gray wall. The driver opened the door of the car. A gate keeper in a white livery stood waiting.

"Get out quickly please," said Mr. Moto. Calvin hesitated.

"Quickly," Mr. Moto said. "It is dangerous in the street." And Calvin got out quickly.

"It is my friend's house," Mr. Moto said. "You are so welcome."

They were in a courtyard and the gate had closed behind them. The courtyard was cool and shaded by a huge matting awning supported on bamboo poles. There was a pool in the center of the court surrounded by potted

113

bushes. A Japanese servant in a white uniform stood before Mr. Moto bowing.

"This way please," Mr. Moto said. "It is nicer than where we were last, is it not? You will like it here so much."

They walked through a round gate in the wall into a second courtyard, and then through another red doorway into a room. The floor was covered with heavy carpets, the chairs and tables were black lacquer and there were pictures of Chinese landscapes upon the wall.

"A very simple room," Mr. Moto said. "My friend has such good taste. They will bring us some whisky in a moment. Ha ha, all Americans like whisky. Sit down, Mr. Gates. The chairs are so very comfortable."

Calvin seated himself beside a small lacquer table and looked about him. The room he saw was used as some sort of office. There was a great flat desk at one end with a telephone and books and papers. A table in the center of the room supported a large map tacked to a board, a military map with colored pins upon it. Mr. Moto smiled and rubbed his hands.

"My friend allows me to work here," he said.

A servant had appeared carrying a tray with bottles and glasses. He placed them upon the table beside Calvin and bowed and smiled and hissed. A second servant followed holding a sheaf of papers which he handed to Mr. Moto. Mr. Moto took them quickly and hurried over to the desk.

"Please refresh yourself," he said. "Ask for what you wish. Excuse, I shall be busy for a little while."

Mr. Moto seated himself behind the desk and read each paper carefully. When he had finished, he placed them in a drawer and picked up the telephone.

"Please pour yourself whisky," he said. "Captain Hamby and Miss Dillaway are on the train for Kalgan. They have no trouble." Then he began speaking into the telephone, in Chinese or Japanese, Calvin could not tell.

He only realized that he was sitting there comfortably, sipping whisky and water, while Miss Dillaway was with Captain Hamby, going where he should have been going. Mr. Moto had said it was nice, but he knew it was not

114

true. The game was not nice which Mr. Moto was playing, if it was not even safe to linger on the street, and it was not hard to see that the game was reaching some sort of crisis. Through the obscurity which surrounded that intrigue and through that ignorance of his, an American's ignorance of the geography and the affairs of the Far East, he was still able to gain a sense of forces taking shape. It was a game for high stakes, where China was involved, and war, and peace. Even as a stranger he could feel the shadow of Japan moving inexorably across the map of China. The shadow was already across Peiping, and moving farther. There was some sort of Japanese army control in Peiping already, and forces were advancing beneath the shadow. Russia was playing a part in it, and the Japanese factions of which Mr. Moto had spoken.

"*Arigato,*" Mr. Moto was saying over the telephone, "*arigato.*"

There was no doubt any longer that Mr. Moto was a very important man. He was balancing those forces as Calvin sat there watching, holding the strings of intrigue in his fingers, pulling this one and that, moving people here and there. He had used Calvin Gates and now he was using Captain Hamby. Before long there would be some sort of denouement when everything would evolve into sinister action. He would not have minded if Miss Dillaway had not been there.

"*Arigato,*" Mr. Moto was saying. He was speaking in a quick, authoritative voice.

"So very nice," Mr. Moto said. "Yes, Captain Hamby and Miss Dillaway are upon the train. You will be so glad to know that the major whom you struck has decided not to kill himself. He is in an airplane now on his way to Kalgan to find Captain Hamby. The young soldiers are so impetuous. So very many things are happening. It seems that your American Embassy is very much upset about your scientific expedition. There is some difficulty, the local prince is holding them. You are so very fortunate to be here, Mr. Gates. I must be leaving in a little while, but you must remain here quietly for a day or two and then you will be quite safe. Matters will be settled in one way or another in a day or two."

Calvin set his glass on the table and stood up.

"Where are you going?" he asked.

Mr. Moto had taken some papers from the drawer and they were rustling softly in his hand.

"So sorry," he said, "I must go north. I have just ordered a plane at the flying field. I must be at Kalgan when Captain Hamby arrives. It is so very important."

Calvin walked across the heavy carpet to the desk and leaned both hands upon it.

"Do you mean you're leaving me here as a prisoner?"

Mr. Moto raised his eyebrows.

"Please," he said, "as a guest not as a prisoner, please. It is only so that you will be safe. Recall, please, what happened to you just this morning, Mr. Gates."

"What's going to happen to Miss Dillaway?" Calvin asked him. "Is she going to be safe?"

Mr. Moto smiled. It was one of those determined smiles peculiar to his race, which had nothing to do with humor.

"Everything possible will be done," he said. "Of course, I cannot be sure."

Calvin Gates leaned his weight more firmly on the desk. Mr. Moto had been polite and almost cordial. He had spoken to him as a guest, but his hospitality did not conceal the truth that Mr. Moto might do anything with him that he chose.

"Please."

"Mr. Moto," Calvin said, "is there anything that might induce you to take me with you? I have to go up there."

Mr. Moto looked and blinked at him.

"You wish to go with me?" he said. "Please tell me why."

Calvin Gates hesitated. It had been difficult for him always to reveal himself to anyone, and before he could bring himself to speak, Mr. Moto continued.

"Excuse me," Mr. Moto said, "it is so necessary to be frank. I wonder why you want to go to Ghuru Nor, a very funny place for one like you to go. You said you were planning to join an expedition. It is not true."

"No," said Calvin, "it isn't true; I gave it as a reason.

116

I've crossed the ocean to go there. There's a man named Dr. Gilbreth, and I have to see him."

"So interesting," Mr. Moto murmured. "Please tell me why."

Calvin's fingers grew white as they pressed against the desk.

"Do not be embarrassed," Mr. Moto said softly. "It will be nicer if you tell me why."

Calvin found that his voice was unsteady. He had given up nearly everything to keep secret what he was now telling. He had believed that he would die rather than speak of it, yet now he found himself speaking to a stranger of another race.

"You know something about it," he said, "because you told me I was wanted by the police. It surprised me very much. I don't know why it should have, except that one does not expect such a gesture from one's family. You said I was wanted for theft, but there's another word for it. It's forgery they want to see me about. I confessed to it before I went away. It's that scientific expedition, Mr. Moto. Dr. Gilbreth was given a forged check of ten thousand dollars. It was honored by the bank."

"Oh yes," said Mr. Moto softly, "yes. I do not understand—you forged the check?"

"I didn't." Calvin choked on his words and cleared his throat. "I took the blame. Someone else did. I'm afraid I'm not being clear."

"So sorry for you," said Mr. Moto. "Why must you see Dr. Gilbreth, please? To prove your innocence perhaps? Surely a communication could have reached him just as well."

Never in his life had he felt so wretched as when he stood there meeting Mr. Moto's glance. In some way his pride was hurt, not that he was ashamed. It was rather that his story had a ridiculous ring when it was put into words.

"He's the only one in the world who will know who forged it," Calvin said. "I've come out here to ask him not to tell. You believe me, don't you?"

"So sorry," said Mr. Moto. "People do such strange things. Will you finish please."

"Oh hell," said Calvin. Mr. Moto's quiet voice seemed to be pulling the words from him. "Maybe I was crazy, I don't know. A girl wrote that check. My uncle's daughter, if you want to know. She was crazy about this Dr. Gilbreth. She was sure to be caught with it. It's a family matter. I didn't do it for her, I did it for the old man. I knew he'd like it better that way. He's always looked out for me and I haven't been such a help. Wild, Mr. Moto, always wild. Never seemed able to settle down, that's the story, Mr. Moto, and you wouldn't have dragged it out of me if you'd cut me to pieces, except that I want to keep on traveling. I don't want to stay here, Mr. Moto."

He felt tired when he had finished, as though he had been through some violent physical effort. Yet he felt better when he had spoken, relieved because he had broken some repression inside his mind. It had not occurred to him before that there might be gentlemen in Japan with feelings like his own until Mr. Moto spoke again. Mr. Moto stood up, clasped his hands in front of him.

"So honored," Mr. Moto said, "so very deeply honored that you should have told me. Gentlemen do such very strange things, even in Japan. So honored, but still I do not understand."

"Understand what?" Calvin asked.

"Why you cannot wait," Mr. Moto said. "In three days—in four days I think, you might see Dr. Gilbreth much more easily."

Calvin Gates stammered and felt his face grow red.

"I can't leave Miss Dillaway up there," he said. "I don't know what's going to happen to her and you won't tell me. I can't leave her like that. I've got to go on. I've got to be starting now."

Mr. Moto placed the tips of his fingers together and hissed respectfully.

"I cannot understand," he said, "which it is you desire the most—to see Miss Dillaway or to see Dr. Gilbreth."

"Does it make any difference?" Calvin asked him.

"Please," said Mr. Moto, "excuse me. It would make a difference to yourself. You would be so much happier if you could make up your mind. It seems to me you are confused. You are willing to add difficulty for yourself be-

118

cause a lady is in difficulty—not a logical reason I am afraid—so much nicer if we know just what we want."

"Logical enough for me," said Calvin Gates.

Mr. Moto glanced up at the painted beams of the ceiling.

"So often," he said, "I have seen such gracious ladies disrupt political combinations." He sighed and still stared at the ceiling seemingly lost in memory. "Such a lovely girl in Washington—I was so much younegr then. She sold me the navy plans of a submarine. The price was thirty thousand yen. When the blue prints came, they were of a tugboat. Such a lovely lady. Such a lovely lady in Tokyo. She took me to see the goldfish in her garden, and there were the assassins behind the little trees. Not her fault but theirs that I am still alive—they were such poor shots. I do not understand lovely ladies, but still I trust them sometimes. First you quarrel with Miss Dillaway and then you wish to find her. I have done the same thing myself, but now I like to think I have learned better. Excuse me, Mr. Gates, you must like Miss Dillaway so very, very much."

Mr. Moto's manner had grown friendly as he confided those details of an earlier life. Perhaps he was telling more about himself than he thought. Calvin saw him for the first time as a lonely sentimental man, moving in a garish world of intrigue and sudden death.

"Yes," he said, "I still trust them sometimes. I hope so very much that this is worth your while."

Mr. Moto's voice seemed to draw speech from Calvin Gates against his will.

"Suppose I do like her very much or suppose I don't," he said, "it would be the same thing. I should want to go away."

Mr. Moto's expression brightened.

"Oh," he said, "I understand so perfectly. It is a code of chivalry. Oh yes, we have a code in Japan, a very careful code. It makes us do so many things we do not have to do. It is why Major Ahara thought that he must kill himself." Mr. Moto sighed. "I am so very sorry that he decided not to kill himself." Mr. Moto's quick bright eyes moved again toward the ceiling. "He is such a very vigorous man, so powerful politically. He represents the extreme military clique and he wants so very much to get that cigarette case. I have been sent by the Government to estimate the situation here and with authority to investigate and direct a certain military operation, and now he is so cross with me because I am conservative."

Mr. Moto smiled deprecatingly and rustled the papers on his desk.

"So nice to have a little talk with you, Mr. Gates. So funny that I should be saying so much to a stranger. I suppose you wonder why."

"I don't believe you do anything without a reason," Calvin said, and Mr. Moto looked very pleased.

"Please," said Mr. Moto, "it was because you expressed a wish to go with me. You might be useful, but it is so necessary for you to understand that everything is so very serious. A human being counts for so very little. I hope you understand."

"I'll do anything you say," Calvin said, "as long as I go on. I don't care what happens after that."

"What happens after that," Mr. Moto repeated. "You mean—there will not be so very much for you after that? It is as though I offered you employment—oh excuse me, please."

A voice at the doorway had interrupted him. It was one of the white-clad Japanese servants, no longer obsequious and polite. The boy had been running and now he spoke with sharp intakes of breath, and the news, whatever it was, could not have been pleasant, for Mr. Moto walked hastily around the desk. He spoke sharply and the boy turned and darted out the door. Mr. Moto's eyes had a sharp beady glint and all expression had left his face.

"Well," Mr. Moto said. "This is not very nice."

"What's the matter?" Calvin asked.

Mr. Moto spoke rapidly, but his voice was still low and soft.

"There are soldiers in the courtyard," Mr. Moto said. "They are coming with the General of Intelligence."

Calvin's hand moved toward his coat pocket and Mr. Moto seized his arm.

"Please," he whispered, "be very careful please. I am

120

so very uncertain—I am not sure whether they want you or whether it is to be a liquidation."

"A liquidation?" Calvin repeated after him.

"It may be that they decide to liquidate me." Mr. Moto's voice was softly insistent. "Sit down where you were, Mr. Gates, and pour yourself some whisky please. You have your pistol in your pocket? That is very nice. A man is coming in, a general. He will not bring soldiers in here with him yet. I shall talk to the general, but give me your attention. If I rub my hands together like this, will you be so kind as to shoot the general very quickly, please."

"Shoot the general?" Calvin repeated.

"Yes," said Mr. Moto, "please. If I rub my hands together—so. It may be so very necessary, and do not hesitate. Do not rise when he comes in. The general is so very nice. If I rub my hands together—so."

Calvin Gates sat down. Mr. Moto was calm enough, but Mr. Moto's calmness set Calvin's heart to beating crazily when he heard the precise click of boot heels on the pavement of the courtyard.

The general was a small man. He paused at the open door and the sun glinted on his spectacles and his belt and riding boots shone brightly. He was in khaki field uniform which fitted him so loosely that he looked more like a professor than a general, a very serious man whose narrow, receding chin and heavy lips were framed by a little black moustache.

He began speaking in a thin high voice as he stepped over the threshold and Mr. Moto advanced, bowing, with his hands clasped in front of him.

"So very nice to see you, my dear sir," Mr. Moto said, "so very, very nice."

Those English words answering the general's native speech puzzled Calvin Gates and they must have puzzled the general also.

"Please," Mr. Moto answered, "we will speak in English. This other gentleman does not understand Japanese, I am so very sorry, and your English, General, is so very, very good."

The general looked at Calvin Gates through his heavy spectacles.

"There is no reason for this," he said. "I came to have a private talk. Why have you brought this man here?"

"Excellency," said Mr. Motto, "this man is here for my own reasons, please."

The general turned toward Mr. Moto and frowned.

"This is not correct," he said. "He has insulted the army."

Mr. Moto clasped his hands together.

"So sorry for you, my dear sir," he answered. "You understand my position here. You have seen the orders please?"

The general's frown grew deeper. There was something venomous in the way he looked at Mr. Moto, as though he were repressing a thousand things which he wished to say and do. He drew in his breath with a sharp, sputtering sound and spoke again in Japanese. His words snapped like little whips and he struck his hands together, while Mr. Moto stood listening.

"So sorry," Mr. Moto answered in English. "So sorry for you, my dear General."

The general swallowed over a word and continued speaking. His narrow face had grown livid. Mr. Moto clasped his hands again.

"So sorry for you, my dear General," he said. "You cannot arrest this man because I have my reasons. So sorry for Major Ahara."

The general drew in his breath again and Mr. Moto pulled a paper from his inside coat pocket. There was a heavy seal upon the corner which Mr. Moto indicated respectfully.

"So sorry for you," said Mr. Moto softly. "I should be so very sad to report that you saw this and disobeyed. I have full control, my dear sir. There can be no doubt about it."

Mr. Moto replaced the paper but the sight of it had changed the general's tone. He appeared to be expostulating when he spoke again. He walked to the table that held the map and began pointing at the pins. Mr. Moto followed him and leaned above the map, but once while the

122

general continued speaking, Mr. Moto glanced toward Calvin Gates and smiled.

"So sorry," Mr. Moto said. "Nothing must move. I understand so well that you are anxious, my dear General. The staff had full directions just last night. So sorry that no troops must move."

The general burst into another torrent of words and emphasized them by beating his fist on the table while Mr. Moto listened.

"So sorry," Mr. Moto said, "that we have different ways of thinking. I understand about the Russian dispositions. Yes. Nothing must move. My humblest regrets. So very sorry."

The general did not speak again. He backed away from the table and glared at Mr. Moto. Then he turned on his heel and walked toward the door. Mr. Moto bowed and stood at the doorway watching while the click of the general's boot heels grew fainter. When he turned back to Calvin his face was wreathed in one of those determined smiles which hid some other feeling.

"The army extremists are so very sensitive," Mr. Moto said. "First it was Major Ahara, and now it is the general. He feels so very much disgraced to have been corrected. I am so very much afraid that he may dispose of himself." Calvin repressed a desire to laugh, because a wild sort of humor was in the situation which combined that bloodthirsty politeness, that composure and petulance.

"If everybody wants to kill himself," Calvin said, "there won't be any army left."

"Yes," said Mr. Moto, "that is very, very true. So many of our most useful people have killed themselves for honor. You think it is funny, and yet you have indicated that you are so very glad to lose your good name."

"I hadn't thought of that," said Calvin Gates.

"Excuse me please," said Mr. Moto, "for calling it to your attention. I am so afraid it will be necessary for you to go with me now. I am so afraid I cannot leave you here, even if I wished. The general might forget himself. I must use you, Mr. Gates."

Mr. Moto's eyes were no longer opaque but deep and calculating. He walked back to the table with its map.

"We must leave here very quickly," he said. "It will not be safe to stay much longer. There is a plane waiting at the flying field. May I ask you to glance at this map? It will interest you I think. Thank you so very much."

Calvin did not know whether to be surprised or alarmed at Mr. Moto's new confiding quality. As far as he could see Mr. Moto had entirely forgotten the confidential nature of his mission, and instead appeared anxious to tell everything, both anxious and insistent.

Calvin Gates stood looking over Mr. Moto's shoulder at a large military map, the legends of which were written in Japanese, but his ignorance of the characters did not prevent his knowing what it represented. Near the bottom of the sheet he could see the city of Peiping and the hard black curve of a railroad running north from it into a mountainous country. Further north the mountains ceased and ended at a huge bare stretch. Mr. Moto tapped it with his finger.

"The Mongolian plateau," he said, "such a very interesting place, a rolling, treeless country. It is where the savage tribes once lived that used to conquer China. You observe that it is not so far from Peiping. The strip beyond the mountains where I place my finger is Inner Mongolia. Beyond it to the north is the republic of Outer Mongolia, which is a Russian puppet state. I hope so much you understand."

"Go ahead," said Calvin Gates.

"It is so very nice," Mr. Moto said, "that you are so very clever. You can see so well without my telling you that Inner Mongolia lies between what we call Outer Mongolia and North China. Now if you please, I must be very, very frank. It is essential for its economic future that the Japanese Empire should dominate North China."

"I have heard you were going to grab it," Calvin said. "Everyone knows that."

Mr. Moto looked surprised and pained.

"That is not a nice way of saying it," he said. "Excuse me, your own great country has taken territory. The British Empire has taken nearly half the globe. Why should not Japan? It is the manifest destiny of stronger nations. Nevertheless, we do not wish to grab. We only desire a partnership, a cordial co-operation, an understanding with the Chinese. We wish to advise and to help them, to develop their resources. I am sure that you are clever enough to understand."

Mr. Moto paused and sighed.

"It is very unfortunate that so many nationalistic elements of the Chinese are so difficult. We have tried so very hard to offer advice and co-operation. We have offered them our army to pacify the country, yet they grow difficult, particularly the American-educated Chinese. If I am rude, I am so sorry."

"They probably want to run their own country in their own way," said Calvin Gates.

"Yes," Mr. Moto agreed. "It is necessary now to convince them that they must co-operate. It is believed in highest quarters that there must be a show of force."

"You mean there's going to be a war?" Calvin asked.

"Please," said Mr. Moto, "hardly that. Nothing more than a military occupation. It is so unfortunate that the great powers do not understand."

Mr. Moto pointed at the map again.

"It would be so unfortunate, for instance, if Russia did not like it. As a result of such a demonstration, Russia might move into Inner Mongolia. It is so important to be sure. Look where I am pointing please. You see that line of hills; it is Ghuru Nor. If Russia decides to move, she will occupy them. Now look over here, please, further to the right. Those little pins represent three divisions of our army on the Mongolian plateau. You heard the general speaking. He is so very anxious to move forward to occupy Ghuru Nor at once as a necessary protection before the demonstration starts."

"I don't blame him," said Calvin Gates.

"Thank you," said Mr. Moto. "You have the military mind. And now we come to the cigarette case, Mr. Gates. The Russian Intelligence have discovered the very day when we propose to make this demonstration. The date is conveyed by the little birds upon the case. Do you mind if I am very frank? There will be an incident the day after tomorrow, Mr. Gates."

Mr. Moto's gold teeth glittered. He appeared delighted at Calvin Gates's bewilderment.

"Then I'm damned if I understand," Calvin Gates blurted out. "You mean you're going to let the Russians get that message?"

Mr. Moto nodded in delighted agreement.

"Yes," he said, "oh yes, that is so exactly. I am so glad for you that you understand. It must have been so puzzling for you. I am so very anxious for a certain Russian official to get the message telling him the exact day and hour, and to be convinced that it is right. He must be certain that it is not a trap. So nice you understand."

Calvin Gates had heard of the subtleties of the Oriental mind, but he could not understand.

"You must have some reason," Calvin said.

"Yes," Mr. Moto said. "Yes, a reason. I am such a humble man, but I am so fortunate to have the confidence of some very great—some august individuals. I speak for a very august individual. You heard me address the general? You see those pins upon the map? The staff has given advancing orders for those little pins. The staff wished those little pins to be moving yesterday toward Ghuru Nor. I have used my authority yesterday to countermand that order. Those little pins cannot move until I tell them, I represent such a very august personage."

"Who's that," asked Calvin Gates, "the Emperor of Japan?"

Mr. Moto looked startled.

"Please," he answered, "I cannot permit you to use the word. I only said a very august personage."

"And you're sending that message in," said Calvin Gates, "and stopping your army from acting."

"Yes," said Mr. Moto. "Please, they cannot act unless I give the order. I want so much for you to understand."

"I don't blame the army for wanting to kill you," said Calvin Gates.

"So nice of you to see," said Mr. Moto. "I am not speaking for nothing. It concerns you so much. We are now in Peiping. In a very few minutes, we shall take a luncheon basket and go to the flying field. A plane will be waiting to take us north. You will observe the city just at

126

the edge of those mountains. That is Kalgan, Mr. Gates. It is where the camel caravans used to start out into Mongolia. It is where Captain Hamby will arrive early this evening. I am so afraid that the army intelligence knows already that Captain Hamby and Miss Dillaway possess that cigarette case. We shall land at Kalgan, Mr. Gates. The field is no good, but we shall land. You follow me so far?"

"Yes," said Calvin Gates.

"Thank you," said Mr. Moto, "so very much. I was so very pleased that Captain Hamby believes I am using you. That is why you are going with me, because I am using you again. I know where Captain Hamby will go at Kalgan."

"And you're going after him," Calvin interrupted.

"Please," said Mr. Moto, "wait. "I am not going after Captain Hamby. You are, Mr. Gates. It is your regard for Miss Dillaway that brings you and also the Captain's offer of three thousand dollars. I am so sure Captain Hamby will appreciate. You are to tell to Captain Hamby all I have told you, and all about my humble self. He wants to know so very much. There is only one thing not to tell him—not what the cigarette case means, please."

"But I don't see what you're driving at," Calvin Gates began.

Mr. Moto's ingratiating smile disappeared.

"I do not ask you to see," he said. "I ask you to do what I say, please. If you do not, you will be so sorry. You have shot a Japanese subject, Mr. Gates."

Calvin Gates grew angry.

"You needn't threaten," he said. "If you want me to tell Hamby what I know about you, I'm glad to do it. But I'd look out for Captain Hamby."

"Thank you," said Mr. Moto, "so kind of you to tell me. It is time to be starting now I think. Please excuse if I was rude. So sorry."

Mr. Moto picked up a small brief case from the desk.

"You're sure you want me to tell Hamby everything?" said Calvin Gates.

"Yes," said Mr. Moto. "So sorry for you we cannot wait for lunch, but there will be sandwiches in the plane."

Calvin Gates was not thinking of food, he was thinking of Captain Hamby, and of Captain Hamby's endless song about the troubles in the old kit bag. Captain Sam Hamby could look out for himself, and Captain Hamby was not a man to be caught in any trap.

"So sorry for *you,* Mr. Moto," Calvin said.

CHAPTER 15

MR. MOTO must have said exactly what he wanted, no more, no less, for his loquacity ceased abruptly and he no longer seemed anxious to discourse upon the economic aims of Japan or upon his nation's manifest destiny.

Nevertheless in the next half-hour Calvin Gates observed that Japan's manifest destiny had reached Peiping. The great northern capital of China, nominally under China's central Government, appeared already to be under Japanese control, and it was obvious even to a stranger that some understanding had been reached between Japanese and Chinese officials which was definite though obscure. The small brown automobile was waiting in the alley outside the house. It started off at high speed the moment he and Mr. Moto were inside and the Chinese policeman directing traffic at the street corners allowed the car to pass without a single interruption.

Out beyond the city walls the car drove to the center of a flying field without a question being asked, straight up to a small cabin plane with its engine already running. Two Chinese attendants who were standing near it hurried to open the doors. A Japanese pilot was waiting at the controls.

As soon as they were inside, and even before they were seated, the engine gave a roar and the plane taxied to the end of the field and turned into the wind. The increased acceleration of the engine made conversation difficult, but Calvin Gates shouted to Mr. Moto.

"You certainly have good service," he shouted.

Mr. Moto nodded and smiled, opened a cardboard box, took a sandwich from it, and passed it to Calvin Gates.

"Too much noise to talk," Mr. Moto called. "Look out the window, it is very nice." Then he took out a map from his brief case and handed it to Calvin. Just as the plane lifted from the ground Calvin looked at his wrist watch; it was half-past two in the afternoon. Mr. Moto had folded his hands and closed his eyes.

When Mr. Moto closed his eyes, he became an ordinary person, a slightly weary Japanese businessman, and nothing more. It was hard to imagine that such an insignificant individual should be engaged in an intrigue, which dealt with war and the rumors of war. He might have been the emissary of an august personage equipped with some portentous sort of authority, but now his mouth was half open, displaying his gold-filled teeth, and his small sharp face was in repose, while Calvin Gates was left, as he had been left before, to make anything he liked of everything which had happened.

Why was he aboard that plane, at all? He was there because he wished to meet a man named Gilbreth and the meeting would ruin him for good. He was there because a girl, whom he had met two days before, and who had no possible claim upon him, might be in difficulty.

If a stranger had come to him and had presented such a case, he would have doubted that stranger's sanity. Yet though he could see himself objectively, logic did nothing to alter the impulses within him which made him face life as though it were a game played by arbitrary and artificial rules. It did no good to realize that he was ruining himself by those rules, even when he could look quite clearly into the future. Before he was finished he would be turned into a shabby sort of adventurer who hung on the outskirts of a disordered world. He was on the road already, watching himself move deliberately along it.

He had the strange feeling of being a partially disembodied spirit, a feeling of being carried rather slowly through the air away from something which had been himself, away from any possible connection with his past or with tradition.

He could see the land below him in a new perspective,

129

much as he saw himself. He had heard so much of the riches of China and of the density of its population that he was surprised by the barren ruggedness of the country. The city of Peiping was growing flat, resolving itself into the mystical plan of its early builders, with the yellow roofs of its Forbidden City and its imperial lakes and gardens set like a jewel in the center of the streets and walls. From the distance, for the plane was climbing higher, the gates and temples and the Drum Tower and Bell Tower all took on the unity of the conception of a single mind. And then they were over a treeless, bare wilderness of mountains, which rose in successive steps away from the plain. He could see the roofs of temples and villages and palaces, a part of some ancient tradition which was as artificial as his own traditions. The country grew more melancholy and rugged, until he was conscious of nothing but a chaotic mass of mountains, which lay beneath them in misty waves almost like a sea, in dusky reds and purples and yellows. It seemed like a barren land hardly worth a struggle, but men had fought over it since the dawn of history.

Mr. Moto opened his eyes and sat up straight; then he touched Calvin's arm.

"Nankow Pass," Mr. Moto said. He spoke impersonally like a guide from Cook's. "A part of the Great Wall of China—very, very interesting."

The wall stretched beneath them over that hilly country like a snake, in an endless succession of curtains and watch-towers, the last and greatest defense between the capital and the barbarians of the North.

"The older wall is farther north," Mr. Moto said, "by Kalgan. Very, very interesting."

The bare, mountainous country beyond the wall glowed hotly in the clear, bright air, as they passed over it with the deceptive slowness of a plane at a high altitude and, beyond another range toward the horizon, he could see the beginnings of a country that was a yellowish, sandy green. He nudged Mr. Moto and pointed.

"Out here?" Mr. Moto said. "Mongolia. We should reach Kalgan in a few minutes now."

Mr. Moto was nearly right about the time. They had

traversed, in hardly more than an hour, a country which had once taken a camel caravan a week to cover.

The plane was losing altitude, descending toward a broad, dusty valley with a rampart of purple hills beyond it. There was a drab-colored city in the valley continually growing clearer—a railroad station, narrow streets, gray-tiled roofs, and large areas enclosed by earthen walls.

"The old compounds," Mr. Moto said, "for the horses and the camels, when the caravans went to Urga. So very interesting." But Calvin was growing weary with unfamiliar sights. Mr. Moto touched his arm again, and pointed out of the window.

"Down there," he said, "is where Captain Hamby will stop when the train comes in—the compound of a company that does business with Mongolia. It is conducted by a gentleman whose name is Mr. Holtz."

Mr. Moto was pointing toward a walled enclosure that looked almost like a fortress. It was toylike from the distance, with figures of men and animals moving behind thick mud walls.

"The Captain stays there always," Mr. Moto said. "Yes—they will be waiting for the cigarette case—so very eager."

His voice was hardly audible because the change of pressure deafened Calvin Gates as the plane descended. They landed in a dusty field which could have been used only for emergencies, but an automobile was waiting for them on the bare brown ground and a dusty, tired-looking Japanese was waiting with it. He spoke to Mr. Moto excitedly while Calvin stood blinking stupidly in the glare of the afternoon sunlight.

"So very nice we got here so quickly," Mr. Moto said. "We shall have an opportunity for a little rest. We are going to the China Hotel, such a nice hotel. Get in the automobile, please."

Calvin did not try to see where they were going, for all sights and sounds had become monotonous and endowed with a peculiar similarity. The hotel consisted of a slatternly courtyard with cell-like rooms that opened off it. An old Chinese in a dirty black gown led them to two narrow, connecting cubicles, each with a bed, a chair and

131

a basin of water, with flies from the courtyard buzzing through open windows.

"This is your room, please," Mr. Moto said. "You will want so much to rest I think. There is nothing to do till sundown, and it will not be nice if you go outside. Make yourself comfortable, please."

Mr. Moto and the Japanese who met them moved into the next room and Calvin Gates listened incuriously to their voices. The buzzing of the flies mingled drowsily with their talk, and the sound made Calvin Gates aware of his own weariness. As he lay down on the narrow bed he felt almost contented. At least he was where he had wished to go. He was very nearly on the edge of no man's land, where civilization as he had known it ended. The city and its walls bore the definite imprint of a Chinese culture but beyond the hills which encircled it he had seen the crumbling mound of China's ancient wall, and there were no more cities beyond that mound, only the yellowish green rolling country, where the plateau of Central Asia began, a space upon which no civilization either of the east or west had made a very permanent imprint. He was at the edge of that blank which Mr. Moto had shown him on the map, over which Japan and Russia both sought to gain control while they eyed each other like wrestlers waiting to come to grips.

It was dusk when he was awakened by a hand grasping his shoulder, and when he opened his eyes, he saw Mr. Moto standing over him.

"So very nice you slept," Mr. Moto said. "I am having tea and sandwiches sent in. It is time you were awake now, please. The train has come. Captain Hamby and Miss Dillaway have arrived."

Calvin Gates stood up, and saw that Mr. Moto's face looked thin and anxious in the dusk. His voice was as soft as ever, but Calvin could detect a vibration of excitement in it.

"You are prepared to do what I told you?" Mr. Moto said.

Calvin Gates looked back at him, but Mr. Moto's expression told him nothing.

"I promised you, didn't I?" he said.

Mr. Moto clasped his hands and bowed.

"It is so nice that I can believe you," he said. "You are like a man in a game of chess. You will just move forward, please."

"Go ahead," said Calvin Gates, "tell me what to do."

"First you will have tea and a sandwich," Mr. Moto said. "You must not be surprised at anything."

"Believe me," said Calvin fervently, "I won't be surprised at anything."

"So glad for you," Mr. Moto said. "There will be a boy waiting for you who will take you to Captain Hamby, please. Captain Hamby will be staying with this merchant who does business with Mongolia. He is Mr. Holtz, part German, part Russian, very fat. Please to remember the name."

"All right," said Calvin, "I'll remember."

"He lives in a place behind great walls," Mr. Moto said. "Matters are so unsettled here that businessmen must protect themselves. You are to go to the main gate; the guide will show you there. You are to beat upon the gate and shout for Captain Hamby. It will be very strange inside, but they will take you to Captain Hamby I think, and then you are to be very frank with Captain Hamby, please, just exactly as I told you, please."

Calvin Gates shrugged his shoulders impatiently.

"You'd better tell me exactly what you want," he said.

"So very glad to tell you," Mr. Moto answered steadily. "Captain Hamby must understand that you have been working for me and that you are finished, please. You have escaped from me. You have heard that he is staying with Mr. Holtz. You do not like me any more, but you have other reasons. You feel there is more money for you by telling him everything that you know about me. You are worried about Miss Dillaway. It will be nice to tell him that, and you must also tell him that white men must stick together. Excuse me, he will understand."

"White men must stick together," Calvin Gates repeated.

Mr. Moto's eyes never left his face.

"You are to tell him particularly that I have full powers over the army, please. It cannot move without me,

133

and be sure to tell him this last. You have just left me at the China Hotel alone. Be sure to tell him that. Are you ready now? You do not look very happy, Mr. Gates."

A watchful look in Mr. Moto's eyes told Calvin Gates that his own expression must have changed, and it was more than an expression; it was a change within himself. He was not the same person who had started on those travels; he was not the same person with whom Mr. Moto had dealt a few hours before. Something had made him see himself entirely differently. Something made his thoughts move erratically, as though he had been awakened from a sleep which had been over him for years. He was very nearly at the end of his journey and yet he was at the parting of some road which lay inside himself.

"Why do you not answer please?" Mr. Moto was saying gently.

But Calvin Gates did not reply. He never knew what sort of person he had been all his life, until he saw himself in that minute's strange illumination; and he saw himself through the ruthless skill of Mr. Moto's mind. No other man had moved him as Mr. Moto had, like a chessman on a board. He had been a marionette that danced while someone pulled the strings; he had never been man enough to seize one of those strings with his own hand and snap it. He heard himself speaking in a thick hushed voice.

"To hell with it," Calvin said.

Mr. Moto's dark eyes grew intent and sharp.

"What?" Mr. Moto asked. "What have you said please?"

"To hell with it," said Calvin Gates. "I am tired of being pushed around."

He could see himself clearly for once. He had prided himself on living by a code and instead he had been moved by loyalty and circumstance, and he had never changed a circumstance. He had drifted aimlessly instead, without applying the independence of his mind to anything in life. He saw himself now in that dingy room with the painful clarity of truth, an ineffective romanticist, and it was Mr. Moto who made him see.

"You can't make me run errands for you." He was

speaking, telling the truth to himself at last. "If I wanted to, I could lie and say 'yes,' but I won't lie. I'm not going to be a part of your ideas. I've been a part of somebody's ideas always, and I know where it's got me. By God, I've never given anything a thought. I've acted like someone in a copybook, taking everything that came, and I say to hell with minding your orders, Moto. I'm going out of here right now, and—so sorry for you if you try to stop me."

"Mr. Gates," said Mr. Moto softly, "I am very much surprised."

"That doesn't bother me," said Calvin Gates. "To hell with you and your Oriental tricks and your majors and your generals, and to hell with Captain Hamby. I told you I would see Hamby, but I won't take your orders. I'm going to do what I want because it suits me not you. I'm going to do what I want for the first time in my life because I want it, and not because it's honorable or suitable."

"My dear Mr. Gates," said Mr. Moto gently, "I think I understand so well."

Calvin took a quick step toward him, but Mr. Moto did not move away.

"There is no need to be impetuous," Mr. Moto said, "because you have discovered something about yourself which was so very obvious. I am here alone, I am not armed. As long as you see Captain Hamby—"

"You heard me," Calvin interrupted him. "To hell with you and Hamby. I'll tell him what I think of you and what I think you're doing, and you can get out of my way right now."

Mr. Moto stood motionless for a moment and then he drew a soft sibilant breath and stepped aside.

"My dear Mr. Gates," he said, "I do not wish to stop you. Excuse me, I might try if I wished, but I am so very happy that you will do what you want. The boy is waiting outside to take you." Mr. Moto paused and smiled. "You see I can only hope that what you want is what I want— so difficult for me."

Calvin Gates scowled at him, but he could not tell whether he liked Mr. Moto or disliked him. He only knew that he understood himself. He was free for a little while at any rate of impulses and inhibitions which had always held him fast.

"I wouldn't be too sure," he said.

CHAPTER 16

MR. MOTO SIGHED.

"It is so very interesting," Mr. Moto said, "to see how people change. I am so glad for you that you are changed, Mr. Gates. I am so happy to think that I may have helped you. Always judge what you want, please, Mr. Gates, before you think what you ought to do. Yes, always try to make events do what you wish them. So glad if I have made you understand. I should be so very honored to shake hands. I intend no trick, believe me, please."

"Why can't you be frank with me, Moto?" Calvin asked.

"Well, never mind. I didn't think that you'd take things this way."

"So sorry that I cannot be frank," Mr. Moto answered. "But I should like so very much to be friendly. I think you are a nice man, Mr. Gates. I should be so honored to shake hands." And Calvin Gates shook hands with Mr. Moto. A Chinese boy in a plain gray gown was waiting outside the door.

"Follow me, please, master," he said softly, and Calvin followed him through the inn gate into a quiet, dusty street. It had grown cool now that the sun was down and the air was fresh and invigorating. The faint light which was still in the sky made all the buildings shadowy and large, and now the dusky strangeness of China, its sounds and smells, and all the ordinary resilience of its life surrounded him. They walked out of the narrow street into a broad, main thoroughfare with banners in Chinese characters strung above it, and with brightly lighted shops on either side, where cloth vendors chanted in singsong voices. Rickshaw bells rang at him warningly. He heard the tinny blare of a radio and the singing of caged birds. They crossed a small stream where women were washing clothes and then they turned from the shops into another narrow street which was lined again with shadowy walls. At the end of a ten minutes' walk his guide stopped at a corner and pointed toward a huge gate, across a narrow street.

"It is there," he said and then he slipped away leaving Calvin Gates gazing at a high mud wall which stretched into the shadows as far as he could see. There was nothing near him but those windowless walls, no light or sign of life, and the gate with a small door for pedestrians cut in one side was like the entrance to a fortress. It all was like some street in the Middle Ages when nearly every house was a stronghold prepared against attack.

He pulled at a string that hung near the door and he heard the deep, sonorous ringing of a bell, and, in answer, a wicket in the door slid open. The darkness in the street, for the light was waning rapidly, made it impossible for him to see anything of the face at the wicket except the glint of eyes. A voice called something to him, and Calvin called back loudly.

"Hamby," he called, "Captain Hamby!" And then he thought of something else that might have significance and added: "Holtz. Ghuru Nor."

When he called to that unseen face at the wicket he had the feeling of shouting in space, a feeling that became a conviction when the opening was slid shut. He seized the rope again and pulled and pulled, and the insistent clatter of the bell chimed in with his anger at himself and at all the net of words and actions which had caught him. Before he knew what he was doing he found himself kicking at the door, and when his foot came in contact with the wood, the door opened inward so suddenly that he nearly lost his balance. He stumbled into a world which was entirely strange.

He was standing in a long, vaulted passage which opened into a dim, open space beyond, large enough to be the parade ground of a fort. The passage was lighted by torches set in brackets, like the torches of some castle gate. On either side of it was a room, carved out of the thick mud wall, and both the chambers glowed with a yellow, uncertain light. The place was reeking with the smell of burning oil from the torches and with the odors of sheep tallow and of rancid butter. In one of the rooms, some heavy men stripped to the waist were putting fuel under a huge caldron where a mutton stew was boiling. The room across the passage was filled with men sitting on their heels, eating with their fingers and chopsticks out of small round bowls. He had a confused glimpse in that flickering light of dark, greasy faces with high cheekbones and flat noses, of oily pigtails and greasy hats, of long-sleeved robes and sashes, of silver amulets and of knives in silver scabbards, and of heavy boots with curved pointed toes. That first glimpse was like a picture out of focus, but it was enough to show him that he had stepped from an ancient, meticulous civilization into a barbarous world, that the gate through which he had passed had opened into Tartary and he was gazing at a group of Mongolians enjoying their evening meal.

He saw those sights only for an instant out of the corner of his eye because his immediate attention was given to two men in front of him. The first was a tall man in a long-sleeved robe with a silver knife in his belt and with heavy boots with up-turned toes, who stood grinning, showing a set of fine white teeth. The second man was more easy to comprehend; when one first saw him he might have seemed someone from a New York street on a hot summer night. He was a very fat German with a shaven head, in slippers, trousers and a shirt that was open at the neck. His heavy paunch shook comfortably when he moved. His small eyes peered through rolls of flesh that fell in heavy jowls around his jaw. His shaven head and his face were glowing with perspiration, and before he spoke he mopped his forehead with a blue bandanna handkerchief.

"Vell," he said. His voice was guttural and was small for his enormous weight. "I'm Holtz. Vat do you want yelling and kicking at the compound gate? Business hours is in the daytime. Vat do you want?"

"I want to speak to Hamby," Calvin Gates said, "Captain Sam Hamby. He came here when he got off the train." Mr. Holtz rubbed his handkerchief hard across his forehead and shouted something at the top of his lungs which made everyone stop talking.

"These Gott verdammt camel drivers," he said. "They will never shut up. You want to see Captain Hamby? Vy do you want to see Captain Hamby? Vat brought you here to see Captain Hamby?"

"I come from Mr. Moto," Calvin Gates said. "I want to see Hamby right away, it's important."

The fat man grunted and his eyes glittered above the pouches of flesh that nearly covered them. His corpulence had not made him good-natured. His mouth was small and his nose like a soft button dividing the expanse of his pinkish cheeks; but he was not good-natured. He spoke to the tall Mongol beside him in a voice which sounded like a high-pitched snarl. The Mongol turned and clattered away in his heavy boots with a horseman's swaying gait, and Mr. Holtz moved his half-concealed eyes back to Calvin.

"All right," he said, "I send to get him. To hell mit these Japanese. They crawl around like sand-fleas. It was bad enough before with war lords, and now come the Japanese." Mr. Holtz spat and grunted. "It gives me a pain in the belly," he added, "one big pain in the belly." Mr. Holtz was not a pre-possessing man, but at any rate Calvin could understand him. He was with one of his own sort again, who was devoid of Mr. Moto's subtlety.

"What is this place?" Calvin asked.

The small lips of Mr. Holtz opened slightly and he emitted a breathing, whistling sound. "It must be so," he said. "So it's your first time out here? You have that look. You are in the compound of Holtz and Company, the same which does business with Mongolia. Ask 'em in Peiping who Holtz is. Ask 'em in Tientsin and Shanghai. Holtz buys everything, every damn thing in Central Asia—wool, antelope horn, wolf hide, Scythian bronze, gold dust, camels, horses, rugs. Holtz is loading camels next week with brick tea, leather goods and textiles. It's damn funny if you never heard of Holtz, my friend."

"It's new to me," said Calvin Gates.

"So," said Mr. Holtz, and it was difficult to decide whether he was genial or sneering.

"New to you, is it? Well, the caravan business is the oldest in the world. It's so antique that it was old when Marco Polo came across the routes. And it's new to you, is it? Well, so what! I think you got a lot to learn from Holtz and Company. Maybe you don't like what you learn when we do business? Huh?"

Mr. Holtz's eyes twinkled icily and his fingers twitched at his waistband.

"It's interesting," said Calvin Gates politely, and Mr. Holtz exhaled another breath.

"So," he said imitating Calvin's voice. "It's interesting is it, to see a lot of Mongol camel drivers, lousy Mongol camel drivers, who haven't washed since they was born, swallowing their supper? Huh? Here is Excellency, Captain Hamby. Interesting? What?"

Captain Hamby walked into the archway from the dim space outside. He walked with a brisk, businesslike step, evidently completely at home, while the Mongol who had gone to fetch him rolled and clumped behind him. Captain Hamby was bareheaded and the light of the torches glinted from his hard gray eyes as he walked forward smiling.

"While you've a lucifer to light your fag," he was humming, "smile, boys, that's the style." And then his song stopped and he looked sharply first at Mr. Holtz and then at Calvin Gates.

"Well, well, well," said Captain Hamby, "only fancy this now. How'd you get here, Gates?"

"By plane," said Calvin Gates.

"Well, well, well," said Captain Hamby, "fancy that." He walked up to Calvin Gates still smiling at him. "And you came here to see me, did you, Gates? And you've met Mr. Holtz? You couldn't have done better. What can I do for you, Gates?"

"I'd like to speak to you," said Calvin Gates, "alone, for about five minutes."

Captain Hamby's face was hard and beaming. "That's fine," he said, "that's fine. A bit busy, but there's always time for a five minutes' chat. Mr. Holtz, this is my acquaintance, Mr. Gates—the one I was telling you about. Shake hands."

Mr. Holtz held out a heavy hand.

"Pleased to meet you, Mr. Gates," he said.

Mr. Holtz was fat but he was very strong. Before Calvin even suspected Mr. Holtz had snatched his hand and had jerked Calvin forward. The next instant Mr. Holtz's arms were around him tight, pressing him against his bulbous, perspiring body.

"Well," Mr. Holtz was saying, "nice to make your acquaintance, what?"

"All right, Holtz," Captain Hamby called.

The arms around Calvin Gates relaxed and Mr. Holtz stepped backwards. Captain Hamby was looking at them grinning. The pistol which had been in Calvin's side pocket was now in Captain Hamby's hand.

"No hard feelings, Gates," Captain Hamby said, "and don't blame Mr. Holtz. My word, he's just all heart. Just take it with a smile, Gates. So you want to have a talk with me?"

Calvin Gates looked from Mr. Holtz to Captain Hamby, and he took it with a smile.

"I'm not fool enough to start shooting here," he said. "I didn't come for that. I've just left Mr. Moto."

Captain Hamby's eyelids flickered. His short square figure was motionless.

"Moto sent you, did he?" he inquired.

"Yes," said Calvin Gates, "and I'm going to tell you why." He glanced around him and back at Captain Hamby's hard, expectant face. Captain Hamby was balancing the automatic in his hand.

"That's fine," he said. "You come along with me." And Captain Hamby put his arm through Calvin's.

"What's the use of worrying," Captain Hamby was humming, "it never was worth while. Tell 'em to wait till I get back, Holtz. Tell the Prince I won't be long."

They walked from under the archway into a huge compound. The last faint light of early evening still fell upon that open space, and the light was broken by the orange glow of torches and lanterns where men were working in the cool, evening air, packing articles into bales and boxes. The place was so unbelievable that Calvin Gates stopped to look. The whole center of the square was filled

141

with camels, row upon row of camels sitting side by side with their long necks arched above their double humps.

"I never saw anything like that," said Calvin Gates.

"No?" Captain Hamby said. "You won't see anything like this a few years from now. It's one of Holtz's caravans, seven hundred of 'em. They're still working on the loads, baling up the brick tea and odds and ends. Holtz wants to get 'em moving off before there's any trouble. Funny-looking beggars, aren't they? Don't get near enough so they can get their teeth in you. A camel's bite can be deuced dangerous. The warehouses are over yonder. It's like loading up a freight train once they load those camels, and the beggars are in good condition too. Look at the humps, all good fat. They'll march six days without food or water; slow, but my word, they're useful where they're going—greatest sight in the world, Gates, something to remember if you come through this."

Calvin walked across the square beside Captain Hamby, as though he were a visitor being taken on a tour, past sweating groups of Chinese who wrapped up tea which had been pressed into large slabs for greater ease in transport, past heaps of embroidered, curved-toed riding boots, past bales of textiles and piles of copper utensils, past the open doors of warehouses stacked high with furs and wool.

"What do you mean by that last remark?" Calvin asked.

Captain Hamby had been humming, and now his humming stopped.

"My word," said Captain Hamby, "you put your neck out, didn't you? Walk on, we're in a hurry. The living quarters are over here."

Still arm and arm, they continued past the warehouses to a group of neat white buildings at the far corner of the compound, the door of one of which Captain Hamby pushed open. It was an office brightly lighted by a gasoline lantern, evidently where the business of Mr. Holtz was transacted. It was strange after the sights outside to be in a room with ledgers and tables and adding machines, and Captain Hamby must have understood Calvin's surprise.

"Holtz's office," he said. "It takes a bit of figuring to run this show." The hard light made the Captain's face jovially harsh. "Well," he said, "go on and talk. Now what's the game, Gates?"

Captain Hamby grew brisk and businesslike and everything about him was genial except the cool glow in his eye. He stood with his hands on his hips, his feet wide apart.

Calvin Gates looked back at him and answered promptly.

"He brought me up here," he admitted, "but I've come here because I want to. I've come here to make you a proposition, Hamby."

Captain Hamby's eyes narrowed, but he still looked friendly.

"That's fine," he answered cordially. "So you thought over what I said on the train? Well, what's your proposition?"

It had seemed simple when he had thought of it, but now he was not so sure.

"A while ago," said Calvin Gates, "you offered me money to tell you what Mr. Moto wanted. I didn't know then, Hamby, but I know now. Is your proposition still open?"

Captain Hamby rubbed his hand sotfly on his coat.

"So you're tired of playing with the Japanese?" Captain Hamby said. "You figure there's more for you in it this way? Is that the picture, Gates?"

"That's the picture," Calvin answered. "I am going to get what I want out of this, Hamby, and you can give it to me and Mr. Moto can't."

It sounded brutally frank as he said it and it showed him how greatly he had changed. All his old compunctions had left him. Mr. Moto had used him and now he was using Mr. Moto. For the first time in his life he was changing circumstances to fit his own desires.

"My word," said Captain Hamby, "that's the sort of talk I like. What is it you want of me, Gates?"

"Nothing that ought to trouble you," Calvin said. "I

143

want you to take me to Dr. Gilbreth. I've come a long way to see him. And I want you to promise that Miss Dillaway is put into Dr. Gilbreth's care. And I want you to arrange that I stay safe with you until this trouble's over. China and Japan won't be healthy for me after this. I'm coming over to your side, Hamby."

"Oh," said Captain Hamby, "I thought you didn't trust me, Gates."

"I don't," said Calvin, "about most things. But I see no reason why you shouldn't do this, because it isn't going to help you not to do it, and it isn't going to cause you trouble. There isn't any other place for me to go. Maybe I'll be useful to you, Hamby."

Captain Hamby nodded thoughtfully.

"You wouldn't lie to me, Gates?" he asked. "My word, if you're lying, you won't live."

Calvin shrugged his shoulders.

"I wouldn't be here if I were lying," he said, "and you know it."

Captain Hamby smiled brightly.

"You must want to see this Dr. Gilbreth a hell of a lot," he remarked. "What's the idea, Gates?"

"That's my business," Calvin answered.

Captain Hamby chuckled softly; he did not appear to be offended.

"Well, well," he said. "Don't be so touchy, Gates. You're talking the way I like a man to talk. Right in my own language. You tell me what Moto wants, and I'll know if it's the truth or not, no fear. And if it is the truth—" Captain Hamby grinned and held out his hand. "I'll do what you want, word of honor, Gates. You'll see Gilbreth, and Miss Dillaway will be put in Gilbreth's care, and you'll come up along with me, and everything is fine. I know how to keep a promise, Gates, no fear. Now what does Moto want? Shake hands."

Their hands met and Captain Hamby's grasp was firm and hard.

"No fear, Gates," Captain Hamby said.

"All right," said Calvin Gates, "I'm going to trust you, Hamby. Mr. Moto's after you."

Captain Hamby rubbed the palms of his hands carefully on the sides of his coat.

"Is that a fact?" he said.

"He wants to get you to the China Hotel," Calvin said. "He wanted me to make it clear to you that he's alone there, but I don't believe it. He's after something, Hamby. He's able to run the whole Japanese army if he wants. I've seen him give orders to a general."

Captain Hamby swung back and forth on his heels. "Smile," he hummed, "smile, smile." And Calvin felt his eyes move over him, examing his clothes and his hands and feet.

"I don't want to be a party to a murder," Calvin said. "Moto's strong on liquidation, Hamby."

Captain Hamby teetered from his toes to his heels and back.

"Damned considerate of you," Captain Hamby said. "My word, I'd never thought of that. Are you telling me he's out from Tokyo and that he's giving orders to the army? My word, I've seen him do that once before. Has he got papers on him? Tell me what you saw, Gates."

Calvin told him while Captain Hamby teetered on his heels and listened.

"My word," said Captain Hamby, "he's got full powers, has he?" He stopped and began humming his favorite tune. "What's the use of worrying," Captain Hamby hummed, "it never was worth while ... My word, you're selling out too cheap. You're either a fool or a damned liar, Gates."

"You can take your choice," Calvin answered.

"I will," said Captain Hamby. "You'll get what you want if it's true. Just step along with me now. Just keep smiling." Captain Hamby linked his arm through Calvin's. "Don't get jumpy, Gates."

"Well," said Calvin, "where are we going?"

"My word," said Captain Hamby, "no need to be so curious. You've been so deuced interesting that I want you to meet more company. Mr. Holtz and the Prince are over yonder. What you have said may change things quite a bit. Now don't get jumpy, Gates."

"What Prince?" asked Calvin Gates.

They were walking toward a brightly lighted building not far from the one they had left and Captain Hamby's hand tightened on Calvin's arm.

"No end obliged to you," he said, "for telling me all this. Puts a fascinating new complexion on matters. What Prince? My dear esteemed patron, Prince Wu of Ghuru Nor. He just came in last night to meet me. You saw some of his laddies by the gate eating mutton. Jolly sort of fellow, the Prince, the sharpest trader I ever knew. Steady's the word for it. Take things as they come and smile."

"Where's Miss Dillaway?" asked Calvin Gates.

"She's all right," said Captain Hamby, "right as rain. Don't get jumpy, Gates."

CHAPTER 17

SOMEONE IN FRONT of the doorway called out sharply, and when the Captain answered a Mongol carrying a rifle stepped out from the shadows.

"The Prince's guard," said Captain Hamby, "one of my boys. Never seen better soldiers. Well, here's Holtzy's house. Does himself rather well. No need of knocking, not a bit of need."

The house was one of those uncompromising, English bungalows, the architectural qualities of which do not vary much, no matter in what part of the world one finds them. Captain Hamby led him into a broad living room furnished with a number of comfortable chairs. He had a glimpse of a table covered with magazines, and of a wall covered with photographs. The room and its furnishings, all so familiar and commonplace, made the people in it the more remarkable. Seated in an oak mission chair, beside a table with a lamp upon it, was a middle-aged man whose whole appearance marked him as an exalted person. His hair was done up tight in a grayish black queue. His cheekbones were high and his dark brown eyes were so narrow that they seemed to be creased in a smile

146

when he was not smiling. His cheeks were gaunt and sunken and a long thin, grayish moustache curled delicately past the corners of a proud, thin mouth. There was no doubt that Calvin was looking at the prince of Ghuru Nor. He was in a gown of turquoise blue, and the pointed toes of his high boots curved upward. He sat erect with a hand resting on each knee, like an ancestral portrait from the Manchu dynasty. Behind his chair were two Mongols, each leaning on a rifle, and a third, a thin pock-marked young man, crouched on his heels at the Prince's right. Mr. Holtz, still in his shirt sleeves, was seated near by drinking a glass of beer, and at the other end of the room four or five more of the Prince's retinue were standing: shiny-faced, glossy-haired young men, leaning on their rifles; but these were not all.

A man in white, seated in a chair near the Prince, had turned to look when the door had opened, and Calvin Gates remembered his face. It was Major Ahara with the saber scars upon his cheek. Major Ahara's heavy mouth had fallen open, and he was starting to rise from his chair.

"Sit down, Major," Captain Hamby said. "Surprised to see this gentleman, aren't you? Your Excellency—this is the American of whom I told you."

The Prince's eyes moved toward Calvin Gates and he nodded.

"I speak English," he said very slowly. "It is all we here can speak together. You go to join Dr. Gilbreth—he did not speak of you."

The slow voice stopped, but not long enough to allow Calvin to answer.

"What is it you want?" the Prince said to Captain Hamby. "We have been waiting."

"Your Highness." The Captain spoke both respectfully and familiarly, like a trusted advisor. "The matter of the cigarette case, Your Highness—it is my advice not to sell it yet."

Major Ahara was leaning forward in his chair listening.

"This Japanese officer has made us a generous offer for it," the Captain went on, "but a situation has arisen. This

147

American has come from Mr. Moto. We must be careful, Your Highness. Mr. Moto is above the army."

The blank expression of the Prince showed plainly that his command of English was not good. He did not understand, but the Japanese major understood, and something in the careful speech caused him to jump to his feet.

"That is not so," the Major cried. "Moto has nothing to do with this, nothing to do with the army!"

Captain Hamby turned on him quickly and spoke in his loud, unmusical voice.

"Sit down," he said. "You Japanese are all alike, always so damn clever. You came here to buy that cigarette case. You flew here from Peiping. We didn't ask you here. Sit down and keep still."

Captain Hamby turned towards Mr. Holtz, who had set his glass of beer upon the floor, and jerked his thumb toward Calvin Gates.

"Holtz, you've got sense," Captain Hamby said. "This man, Gates, Moto sent him. Moto—the one who was here before—and he's in the China Hotel. Well, I'm going out to find him. Moto's been sent direct from Tokyo to give the order to the army. My word he has—and we can't let this go."

Mr. Holtz pursed his lips.

"These Japanese," he said. "My dear friend, it is a trap—perhaps."

Captain Hamby grinned.

"It won't be a trap," he said, "if I bring a handful of my boys."

Mr. Holtz rubbed his hand across his mouth.

"You don't never stop, my friend," he said, "when there's money."

"Righto," said Captain Hamby. "Too right." He whirled around to Calvin Gates. "He was alone, last you saw of him, wasn't he?"

"Yes," said Calvin Gates, "he was alone."

"My friend," said Mr. Holtz, "I should be careful. Why should our dear friend Mr. Gates be here with such a story?"

Captain Hamby grinned.

"Because Moto couldn't come here himself," he answered. "Bloodthirsty devils, the Japanese. Like us not Moto knows he'd be assassinated if he showed his nose in the street. It's their army and their conservatives fighting. Subtle little beggars, the Japanese, always doing things hind end before. He doesn't want Ahara to get that cigarette case. My word, Moto's got some scheme."

Major Ahara pulled himself out of his chair a second time.

"It has nothing to do with the present situation," Major Ahara said. "Mr. Moto is a very bad man, very dangerous. Remember, if you please, the Japanese army will control this country in a very little while. The Prince will do well to respect the Japanese army. It will be better for everyone. I am offering a price for that cigarette case—ten thousand dollars gold—and a further sum for immediate occupation of Ghuru Nor—"

Captain Hamby's grin grew broader. He was evidently enjoying the situation, and the blank expression of the Prince, the sly watchfulness of Mr. Holtz. He was reading something between the lines and Calvin was more sure than ever that Hamby was no fool.

"You're offering money because you couldn't get it any other way," Captain Hamby said. "My word, you tried."

The Major's face twisted with a sudden spasm of temper. Although he controlled his facial muscles, his eyes were glowing.

"It will be better for you to take my offer," he said. "There are other things that I may do."

"Is that a threat?" Captain Hamby asked.

"Yes," the Major said in his guttural English, "that is a threat."

Captain Hamby laughed.

"My word," he said, "you Japanese johnnies are getting insolent. You're talking to a white man, Major—to an army officer, and a damned sight better one than you'll ever be. I don't give sixpence halfpenny for your army. Maybe we'll sell you that cigarette case and maybe we won't. Sit down, Major. We haven't talked to Russia yet."

Major Ahara did not sit down.

"I shall leave here at once," he said.

"Oh no you won't," said Captain Hamby. "You'll sit down and take it easy, Major."

The Major glanced about the room, shrugged his shoulders and sat down, but his eyes never left Captain Hamby's face.

"You are making a very great mistake," he said. "You insult the Japanese army."

Captain Hamby did not appear impressed; neither did the Prince, who still sat with his clawlike hands resting on his turquoise knees, nor Mr. Holtz who had folded his hands across his stomach.

"To hell with the Japanese army," Captain Hamby said. "Two Russian army corps would whip you."

Mr. Holtz raised a hand and dropped it limply on his knee.

"My dear friend," he said, "there is no reason to be insulting. Major Ahara is a nice gentleman. He has offered as a sum of money, not much, but he may offer more, and you are keeping us all waiting. What is it that you wish to do?"

Captain Hamby stepped up to Mr. Holtz and leaned over his chair.

"We don't go ahead," said Captain Hamby slowly, "until I see Moto."

"My friend!" expostulated Mr. Holtz.

"Wait a minute," said Captain Hamby. "Listen to me." And he leaned forward and whispered.

The whisper made the heavy body of Mr. Holtz grow taut and his eyes move forward through the wrinkles in his face like a crab's.

"My friend," said Mr. Holtz, "I never thought of that. No, you never stop where there is money. You had better tell the Prince."

"I'll tell him," said Captain Hamby. "His Highness is a sporting gentleman."

Then Captain Hamby spoke to the Prince in a tongue which was neither Chinese nor Japanese and the Prince answered in sharp interrogation. Captain Hamby looked back at Mr. Holtz.

"I told you," he said, "His Highness was a sporting gentleman."

Mr. Holtz moved restlessly and the chair creaked beneath his weight.

"I do not like it, Captain Hamby. Why do you trust our dear friend, Mr. Gates? Why do you think he tells the truth?"

Until his name was mentioned, Calvin had not realized how absorbed he had been. He had been trying hard to piece together what was behind the words.

"I'll take a chance on his telling the truth," Captain Hamby said. "Moto's alone at the China Hotel, isn't that right, Gates?"

"I told you he was," said Calvin Gates, "and I told you it's a trap."

"That's fine," said Captain Hamby, "that's just fine. You wouldn't be fooling me, would you, Gates? I'm depending a lot on your word. I'm going up to the China Hotel, and if I'm not back here in an hour, you're going to be shot."

"What are you talking about?" said Calvin Gates.

Captain Hamby looked at him hard.

"If I'm not back here in an hour it will mean you haven't told the truth, and you're going to be shot. We haven't time to be gentle tonight."

Calvin Gates glanced across the room and met the Prince's smiling eyes.

"Are you trying to frighten me?" Calvin asked.

"My word no," said Captain Hamby, "I'm just giving you the facts. You're in the middle of a serious business conference. The Prince is trying to decide whether to sell out to Russia or Japan. If I don't come back you won't be alive to know it. Anything you want to say? It's a fair proposition, isn't it?"

"And suppose you do come back?" said Calvin Gates.

Captain Hamby laughed.

"That's the way to talk," he said. "I've always liked you, Gates. My word, if I come back, you won't lose. The Prince will give you a cut-in, and I'll let you out to see the fun and I'll keep my promise. You only have to wait an hour." The Prince had pushed himself out of his chair and was standing, a gaunt, oldish man in a silk gown,

151

leaning an arm on the shoulder of the attendant who had crouched beside him.

"Easy," said Captain Hamby, "don't get jumpy, Gates. I don't want to see Mr. Moto. I want to bring him here alive, and I'll get him if you've been accurate. Anything you want to say?"

Calvin Gates did not answer. Major Ahara shouted something and two of the Prince's guard seized him by the shoulders and pushed him back into his chair. The Prince called out an order and two more of the oily-faced men walked toward Calvin Gates.

"Take it easy, Gates," said Captain Hamby. "They're only going to lock you up. Take it easy, Gates."

Hands were on his arms and he was being pushed towards the door.

"While you've a lucifer to light your fag," Captain Hamby was humming, "smile, smile, smile."

Captain Hamby's humming stopped and his voice made the two guards who were escorting Calvin pause curiously.

"Just one thing while I'm gone, Holtz," Captain Hamby said. "You'd better get General Shirov and test the wireless. Tell Shirov we've got two Japanese. We'll have to settle this tonight."

A hoarse cry from Major Ahara interrupted him.

"You will not dare to do this," the Major shouted. "I will not stay here to face a Russian. You gave your word that this would be confidential."

"Well, well," said Captain Hamby and he looked both surprised and hurt. "Haven't you Japanese ever broken your words? You're talking to Captain Sam Hamby, who is negotiating for Prince Wu of Ghuru Nor. The Prince knows that he has to sell out either to Russia or Japan. He doesn't want to sell out to the wrong party and have his land overrun by the other party's army. We're going to get this matter settled once for all, right here tonight. We don't want any mistakes."

"There will be no mistake," said Major Ahara earnestly. "When I leave here I can assure you that orders will be given to occupy Ghuru Nor."

152

"That's fine," said Captain Hamby, "fine—when you leave here."

If Major Ahara made any response, Calvin Gates did not hear it, because his guards led him out of doors. Both of his arms were gripped tight, but the guards were not rough. He walked silently between them across a corner of the compound toward one of the warehouses which were built against the wall.

He was thinking of what Captain Hamby had said— that anything could happen in China; and now he was sure of it. If he had not seen it he would not have believed it possible that Captain Hamby or anyone else would dare to make such an attempt. It had the effrontery of banditry and the skill of diplomacy. Captain Hamby and the Prince of Ghuru Nor had made the camel compound into a small armed camp with Mr. Holtz to help them, and now in that temporary security they were estimating with whom it might be safer to deal, with Russia or Japan. A feeble Mongol chieftain was balancing two great powers, one against the other, a dangerous enough game and Calvin admired the Captain's skill. Undoubtedly he had been negotiating with both those powers, and now he was holding that cigarette case before them, watching as they both reached towards it. Calvin would have enjoyed that game of wits if he were not involved in it, but the guards walking beside him and the aura of grease and smoke which came from them reminded him that he was not a spectator, but a hostage for Captain Hamby's safety. Although it would do no good to kill him, there was a primitive sort of justice about the idea which would appeal to the Prince of Ghuru Nor.

They were leading him toward the closed door of a warehouse where a sentry stood with a rifle. One of his guards spoke a word of explanation. Then the door was shoved open a crack and Calvin Gates was pushed into an empty barnlike room, lighted with a single horn lantern which hung from the rafters. As the door slammed shut behind him he had an impression of a dry, strong smell of wool and of half-cured hides. He blinked for a moment at the feeble yellow light before he realized that he was not alone, and then he saw that he had nearly reached the

153

end of his journey. He blinked again and cleared his throat.

"Hello, Dillaway," he said.

CHAPTER 18

MISS DILLAWAY had been sitting on a packing box, and now she was on her feet hurrying toward him.

"Calvin," she called, "Calvin Gates!"

He knew that she was glad to see him and she was not angry any more, but what surprised him was his own pleasure at seeing her. It was as though nothing else mattered. Something about her made his heart pound in his throat. She was not even pretending that she was not glad to see him. She had forgotten to be brisk and casual, just as she had forgotten once before.

"Hello, Dillaway," he said again. "I've come to get you out of this."

"Have you?" she answered. "You're the only one I know who'd be fool enough to try." But the edge had left her voice. At first he thought she was laughing at him, and then he saw she was not.

"I'm afraid," she said, "I've been so damned afraid."

"It's going to be all right," said Calvin. "We'll get out of here. Nobody's going to hurt you. It might be a whole lot worse."

"I've been so damned afraid," Miss Dillaway said, "and I don't like it, and I wouldn't admit it to anybody else but you, and I suppose you're pleased."

The old sharpness was returning to her voice, but still he felt contented, because it told him that he had brought her confidence. She had as good as admitted that there was something in those qualities of his which she had ridiculed.

"I'm awfully glad to see you," Calvin said. "I never knew I'd be so glad."

His remark sounded futile. He reached toward her and touched her shoulder.

154

"Dillaway," he began, "if we ever get out of this——"

She pushed his hand away, but she held it tight for a moment.

"If we ever get out of this, I'm going to keep an eye on you," she said. "You need some sort of a guardian. I've been hearing about you, Gates. Don't you see who's in here with us? Don't you see Dr. Gilbreth?"

He had not noticed anyone else since he had set eyes on her, but now he saw a short, stocky man standing near them in a rumpled gray suit.

"Hello, Gilbreth," he said, "what are you doing here?" He was scarcely surprised, because nothing any longer surprised him, but there was the man whom he had traveled halfway around the world to meet, and whose face had not been wholly out of his memory for a long time. Somehow he had expected it to be changed, but there it was exactly as it had been in the past, and not such a very distant past either. There was Dr. Gilbreth, the eminent scholar, the lecturer and explorer, staring at him and making the past the present. There was the same long nose, the same thin grayish hair, the same long weak and studious mouth, and Calvin Gates had his old sense of amazement as to what a girl who was young and good-looking could ever have seen in such a man. He certainly did not look well then. He was no longer a dinner guest, talking about his travels; he was dirty and haggard and his face was covered with a stubble of beard.

"What am I doing here?" he said. "I'm in a den of thieves, and so are you—in case you don't know it. The Prince—have you seen the Prince?—have you seen Captain Hamby? They're holding the whole expedition up for ransom. They've made me cable for funds. I'm going down with Hamby to the bank to draw them tomorrow morning. Don't ask me if there isn't anything else I can do. There isn't except to pay up and get out. There isn't any way to get help. There isn't anything. It isn't any joke, Gates. The Prince means business."

"I guess he does," said Calvin. "He seems like a very remarkable man."

"He means business," said Dr. Gilbreth. "I thought I knew how to handle the natives. Everything was quiet

155

enough in Mongolia two years ago and now it's anarchy. What did they throw you in here for, Gates?"

Calvin Gates shrugged his shoulders.

"It's Captain Hamby's idea," he said. "It looks as though the American flag won't do much good tonight, but I'm grateful to Hamby just the same. I wanted to see you, Gilbreth, and he promised I would. He's kept that part of his promise."

Dr. Gilbreth looked surprised. He looked at Calvin Gates and looked away.

"I don't understand you," he said. "You're not serious when you say you came all this way to see me personally. Wouldn't a letter or a cable have done just as well?"

"I don't think so," Calvin Gates answered. He was reaching the point at last and with it the end of his journey. Yet now that it was time to speak he had his old desire to remain silent. "It's a delicate matter," he said. "It concerns our family. You can help us, Dr. Gilbreth."

Dr. Gilbreth looked puzzled. Calvin wondered if the Doctor understood. He was trying to think of some method of putting everything delicately, but he could think of none.

"You mean your family sent you out to see me?" Dr. Gilbreth asked. "I don't understand. There was absolutely nothing—"

"I don't blame you for being surprised," said Calvin Gates. "We're such a long way from where we started, aren't we? It's hard to think back that far. They didn't send me, I came out myself."

"But why?" said Dr. Gilbreth. "I don't understand why."

Calvin Gates hesitated, still trying to choose words.

"Please excuse me for being so slow," he said. "It's rather hard to talk about. I'd give a good deal if I didn't have to. When you were raising funds for your expedition out here, we were all interested, you remember." He paused. It was not necessary to go into the details, because there was no doubt that Dr. Gilbreth remembered a good deal more than had been mentioned.

"You can't do things like this without money," Dr. Gilbreth said.

"I know," Calvin Gates agreed. "I don't criticize you. I'm not blaming you—for being interesting."

Dr. Gilbreth looked embarrassed.

"Go ahead, Gates," he said. "I know you're talking about that check."

"How do you know," Calvin asked, "that I'm talking about a check? Have you heard anything about it?"

"Never mind," said Dr. Gilbreth. "I want to know what you're getting at."

"All right," said Calvin, and his own voice reflected the other's impatience. "My cousin, Bella Gates, gave you a check as a contribution to your funds. I wish it hadn't been so large, but it was, ten thousand dollars. She got it for you because you said you needed that money very badly."

"I wish I hadn't put the thing so strongly," Dr. Gilbreth said. "I never intended—"

"Never mind about that," said Calvin. "I'm not criticizing and there's no reason to come to personalities. I don't care what she said to you, or what you said to her. She gave you a check for your expedition which was signed by her father. He's my uncle, Dr. Gilbreth, and I think a great deal of him. I'd like you to remember that. That check was honored by the bank. It's no concern of yours at all." He paused again. He did not like to appeal to Dr. Gilbreth or to anybody else, and he went straight ahead, no longer trying to choose his words.

"On the first of the month when the vouchers came in, that check was found to be a forgery, and that's why I'm here. I announced that I had forged that check before I left." He paused again and cleared his throat. "It came as rather of a shock, and now it looks as though the bank has taken the matter out of the family's hands. The authorities are investigating. You're certain to be asked questions because you know more about the circumstances. It's a delicate matter. We think a good deal of the family and my uncle brought me up, and he's had to put up with a good deal from me. When you are questioned I want you to say that I am the only one who could have forged that check. I can give you all the details, but I want you to be positive."

157

He waited, but Dr. Gilbreth did not answer, and Calvin Gates continued.

"You told us you couldn't be reached by cable for three or four weeks at a time," he said, "and I hope you were correct. When I left to come here I thought this whole business would be a skeleton in the family closet and the least said the better. Something must have happened back home. It seems this isn't the first time that there's been a forgery. I only found out the other day that the police at home were looking for me. It made it all the more important that I should see you. I didn't think the old man would do anything like that. He must have lost his temper. You have been out of touch, haven't you? You haven't heard anything about it? I'm taking my medicine for this, and I want to be sure I take it. From everything I've seen, they don't bother much about forgers here."

Dr. Gilbreth was blankly silent. He started to speak and checked himself, and stared at Calvin Gates as though he had encountered an entirely new member of the human species.

"But you didn't," he said. "I know you didn't forge it and I know who did."

The time and the place made no difference now that he and Dr. Gilbreth were face to face. He was living again in a world which he was leaving forever, where nothing had mattered much but manners and security.

He was living through a good part of his past in the silence that followed. His mind moved through days and nights that were irrevocably gone before he answered.

"You're mistaken," said Calvin, "I did it," and then he added a remark which might have been inconsequential if both of them had not understood. "She was crazy about you, Gilbreth."

Dr. Gilbreth still looked at him as though he were an unknown type of human being excavated from the ruins of some vanished civilization.

"I don't understand you." Dr. Gilbreth's voice was embarrassed and incredulous. "I'm damned if I understand what you want. It's embarrassing to me. No matter how you look at it, there's going to be talk, but it had nothing to do with you. Do you mean to stand here seriously and tell me that you came out to this God-forsaken place in order to get me to help you to ruin yourself? There's no one alive who would do such a fool thing as that. I won't believe it. I can't believe it, Gates."

Miss Dillaway's voice chimed in suddenly.

"Well, I believe it," she said. "It's just the sort of thing he would do. It's just the sort of chance you'd jump at, isn't it, Gates?"

He had not intended anyone to hear that conversation. When all his motives were analyzed by an outside mind they appeared almost ludicrous, and besides it was a matter between himself and his own conscience. Now that he had spoken to Gilbreth, he had committed himself once and for all. He had been tempted not to, ever since he had seen Miss Dillaway, but he had spoken.

"This is something you don't know anything about," he said. "For once in my life I've finished something I started."

"Oh yes, I understand," said Miss Dillaway. "We were talking about you, Gates."

Dr. Gilbreth's face was still incredulous.

"But you haven't any motive for doing such a thing," he said. "You didn't even like her. You two hardly spoke."

"Does it make any difference?" Calvin answered. "That's entirely up to me. I did it for the old man, if you want to know. I don't amount to much back home, but I think a lot of him. It's better this way."

There was a silence, as though no one could find an answer, and the silence was so long that Calvin spoke again.

"I suppose you think I'm a fool," he said, "but it doesn't matter. After all, that's up to me. It's the first positive thing I've ever done. That's something."

He had said as little as possible, for it was a subject which did not bear discussion, and yet he had an uncomfortable feeling that he had said everything, and perhaps too much.

"You're not a fool," said Miss Dillaway. There was a catch in her voice like laughter, but she was not laughing. "And I wouldn't have you different. The only trouble is that you need someone to look out for you. You're just not a type that can walk around alone. And for once in your life you're too late. You'd better tell him, Gilbreth."

Dr. Gilbreth hesitated.

"Go ahead," said Miss Dillaway, "tell him, Gilbreth."

"I was reached by cable a week ago," Dr. Gilbreth said. "I didn't know you were coming out here, and I'm glad I didn't know. I wired the facts in self-protection." Dr. Gilbreth shrugged his shoulders. "Maybe I'm not a gentleman. Maybe it's better not to be. And I got an answer back before the wires were cut. I've got it in my pocket. You can read it if you like."

He handed Calvin Gates a piece of paper on which a few words were scrawled in pencil.

Your communication explains situation here stop have taken measures stop rely on your discretion stop to save scandal have stated I signed check and bookkeeper lost record stop authorities accept this explanation stop communicate this my nephew worried about him stop should have consulted me first tell idiot return at once funds forwarded him at Shanghai Roger Gates.

As Calvin stared at the sheet of paper the whole affair assumed an artificial quality—as though it had all been done by someone else.

"I'm sorry," he said slowly, still staring at the paper. "It would have been better if he hadn't known."

"Would it?" said Dr. Gilbreth. "How do you know it would? At any rate, it's over now, and there's nothing you can do."

"Think of that," said Miss Dillaway. "Nothing you can do." He thought that she was laughing at him, but again she was not laughing.

Now that it was finished he could see his whole course of action objectively, as though someone else had taken it, and it seemed quixotic and absurd, like something he might have done when he was much younger. He could not even remember what there had been about it that had once stirred him so deeply. His impulse no longer had va-

160

lidity; instead he discovered something close to egotism in his ideas of family and of honor.

"Dillaway," he said, "I think I'm getting tired of chivalry."

"Well," said Miss Dillaway, "it's time you were."

CHAPTER 19

"ANYWAY," he said, "I met you, Dillaway, and I'm going to get you out of this."

"There you go," said Miss Dillaway, "starting out again."

Calvin Gates stared about the bare, dimly lighted shed. He had half forgotten where they were, until she made that last remark.

"Don't worry," he said. "I'm through with that, and I'm through with being what I was."

Dr. Gilbreth had begun to pace up and down the shed.

"Haven't we talked enough about you?" he inquired. "What's going on out there? What are they trying to do?"

Calvin looked at his wrist watch without answering.

"What's the matter?" Miss Dillaway asked. "Have you got an appointment, Gates?"

"I may have," said Calvin Gates, "in about five minutes." He did not wish to enlarge upon the subject, and he did not wish to be asked questions. "So you gave Hamby the cigarette case? I wish we had it now."

"Well, you can have it if you like," she answered.

"Not here," he answered. "Don't say that. It isn't even funny—if I could get my hands on that case—"

"I mean it," she said. "I've got it if you want it. It's right here in my purse."

She opened her purse and handed him the cigarette case. There it was in silver and black with the same birds that he remembered.

"But why didn't he take it from you?" Calvin cried. He knew Captain Hamby well enough to know that he would not have hesitated.

161

"I thought it might be useful, that's why I kept it," she answered. "Captain Hamby isn't so clever."

"But how did you keep it?" Calvin said. "I don't understand."

"It isn't being very bright if you don't," Miss Dillaway retorted. "Don't you remember that I had a cigarette case of my own, which I bought in Tokyo, with the same type of inlay—that's the one I gave him. Why are you looking at it that way? It won't burn your fingers."

As he stood there staring at the piece of silver his hands began to tremble. It was so completely unexpected that he could not think consecutively. She stood looking at him with a grim sort of triumph and with her old air of superiority.

"I'm not such an idiot, you know, Gates," she said.

"I never said you were," he answered, "but I never thought of this."

"Well, try to think back," said Miss Dillaway. It's simple enough. When Boris offered me that cigarette case on the train you heard me tell him I had a case of my own."

"Yes," said Calvin, "I remember."

He could remember quite clearly now that she mentioned it, but the very simplicity of what had happened made it the more surprising. He stared at the cigarette case and back at Miss Dillaway again.

"Don't you believe me?" she said impatiently. "There it is."

"But why didn't you give him this one," he asked, "when Hamby asked you?"

She gave her head a quick, impatient shake.

"Because I didn't like the way he asked for it, if you want to know," she answered. "He was so sure he was going to get it that he didn't even bother to be polite. He didn't even bother to be impolite, either. I suppose you think that women aren't much use, Gates. That's what most of you romanticists think. You needn't act as though you wished you had thought of it yourself. If you want it, there it is—a present. Aren't you going to thank me?"

"I'm sorry," he said. "I haven't got time. I'm sorry. I'm

trying to think. I want to remember every detail on this case."

The whole thing was completely in keeping with her character. She had always said that she could look out for herself, and she had come very close to doing it. It was as though he had drawn a card to fill a poker hand when the last of his money lay upon the table, and she had given him the card. She had given him a key to let them out of prison. It was better than the bargain he had made with Hamby. If that failed, the cigarette case was still in his hands.

"What do you think I'd better do with it?" he asked.

"I don't know," she said, "that's up to you. I can't do anything, can I, Gates?"

"Well, what's so queer about it?" Dr. Gilbreth said. "It's only a cigarette case, isn't it?" Dr. Gilbreth did not understand, and there was no necessity to explain. Calvin held the cigarette case, and looked at it, until each detail of the design was clear in his memory. Then he opened it and with a sudden wrench he tore the inlaid cover from its hinges.

"What are you doing?" he heard Miss Dillaway ask, but instead of answering he bent the silver cover between his hands. It was a delicate but unstable piece of silver-work. The brittle iron of the inlay snapped as he bent it and bits of it fell to the earth floor at his feet.

"Pick those pieces up," he said to Miss Dillaway. "Hide them somewhere, each one in a different place. Break them first. Bend them out of shape."

He bent the silver in his hands until it broke and then he bent the pieces and broke them again; finally he ground each piece beneath his heel into a shapeless mass. There was nothing left when he had finished.

"They can't put that together," Calvin said, "not if they work a week."

"But what are you doing it for?" Miss Dillaway asked.

"Because I want to get you out of this," Calvin answered. "And no matter what happens—we've got them now, I think."

"But I don't see—" she began, and Calvin Gates stopped her. He was listening to a sound outside.

"Wait," he whispered. "Don't speak, don't say anything."

There was a stir outside the door. It was Captain Hamby. Calvin could hear him humming.

"What's the use of worrying, it never was worth while."

The heavy door creaked open and he stepped inside the shed.

"Hello," said Captain Hamby. "Everybody comfortable? Now don't start complaining. You're all lucky so far."

"Look here, Hamby—" Dr. Gilbreth began.

"Now, now," said Captain Hamby, "that's enough from you, Doctor. You're a secondary problem. You're wanted at the house, Gates. Come along now, come along. My word, this is quite a night."

"So you're back, are you?" Calvin asked. "I suggest you let us all out, Hamby."

Captain Hamby laughed—the laugh of a man in excellent spirits. Whatever the Captain had done since Calvin had seen him last must have been both agreeable and successful.

"Let everyone out!" Captain Hamby made an exaggerated gesture of surprise. "Now, now, that don't come into the bargain, Gates. I'm surprised that you should suggest it, an accurate man like you. Maybe my mind's failing, but I don't recall of talking of letting Miss Dillaway out. I promised to put her under the care of Dr. Gilbreth. Well, she is under his care, isn't she? It isn't my fault if his care don't amount to much. It isn't my fault if he's in trouble with the Prince. Keep your shirt on, Gates."

"You're an Australian, aren't you?" Calvin said. "I forgot your family came out on a convict ship."

Captain Hamby bit his lip and then he smiled again.

"And who are you to talk?" he said. "I don't bite the hand that feeds me, Gates, and you turned up Moto good and proper. I'm not yellow dog taking Japanese pay. Stow it, Gates, don't move."

"That's a lie," Miss Dillaway called out. "He never did that and you know it."

"Never mind it, Dillaway," Calvin said. "There's nothing I'm ashamed of."

"Isn't there?" said Captain Hamby. "Well, that's fine. And there's nothing I'm ashamed of either, when I deal with a new chum like you. I don't know what your lay was, Gates, but it don't make much difference now. You stow it. I'm keeping all of my bargain that I can. I'd promised you you'd talk with Gilbreth, didn't I? You've got a sight more than you deserve, my boy."

Calvin measured the distance between himself and Captain Hamby and leaned forward. Captain Hamby put his hands in his coat pocket and took a quick step back.

"Get some sense in your head, old chum," Captain Hamby said, "and no more of your bloody insults either. If I finished you off right here, nobody would mind. Instead I'm doing what I can for you. Are you coming with me, or do you want me to call some of my boys to drag you?"

"Don't bother," said Calvin, "I'm coming."

Captain Hamby's irritation vanished.

"That's fine," he said. "I've got nothing against you personally, Gates, upon my word. I'll do all I can for you. Just smile, smile, smile. Step ahead of me, smartly now."

Captain Hamby hummed beneath his breath about the lucifer and the old kit bag, as he walked beside Calvin Gates across the compound with two attendants close behind him.

"Just take things as they come, Gates," said Captain Hamby soothingly. "My word, this is none of my doing, it's only your own tight corner, but I promised you'd see the fun. Yes, it's quite a night. It isn't always things work out this neatly. While you've a lucifer to light your fag—"

"Who wants to see me?" Calvin asked.

"Just smile, smile, smile," Captain Hamby said. "A Russian gentleman wants to see you. My word, I'm sorry, Gates. He thinks you murdered a pal of his in that hotel in Mukden. The Prince is allowing him to dispose of you, but I'll do what I can. My word, Gates."

"Never mind your word," Calvin said.

"That's fine," said Captain Hamby, "that's the sporting way to take it. I'll see that Miss Dillaway and the Doctor get back to Ghuru Nor. Maybe they'll get home sometime if they're lucky. We can't suit everybody these days.

You're seeing the beginning of a war. Just between friends, the Prince is near to selling out to Russia, Gates. Just keep smiling. Here we are."

Mr. Holtz opened the door of his bungalow.

"So," he said to Captain Hamby, "here you are."

Everything in Mr. Holtz's room was much as Calvin had left it. The Prince was back in his chair at one end of the room, beside the table with the lamp upon it. Only when Calvin was in the center of the room was he aware of a strained, hushed sort of expectancy, and then he saw the reason. Seated in a stiff-backed wooden chair near the Prince was Mr. Moto.

CHAPTER 20

THERE WAS A GASH on the side of Mr. Moto's head and his coat was torn, but his eyes were bright and steady. His eyes turned toward Calvin Gates and then back across the room where he had been gazing before, straight at Major Ahara.

"Well, well," said Captain Hamby, "there's your old friend, Mr. Moto, Gates. Anything you want to say to Mr. Moto?"

"No," Calvin answered, "except that I told him to look out for you."

"It is all right," said Mr. Moto gently. "Please believe I do not blame you, Mr. Gates. I am so afraid that there is so much trouble."

"Yes," said Captain Hamby, "so much trouble. Gates, here's the gentleman who wants a word with you—over by the table. His name is General Shirov."

A man at the table close to where the Prince was seated turned around in his chair. He was a pale, youngish man with a sharp, studious face. He was holding some papers in his hand, and in that moment as Calvin watched him he wondered if he had not seen the face before; then he realized what had given him the notion, for the man called General Shirov was like the Russian whom

166

he had first seen on the train. He had the same cut to his clothes and the same high forehead and the same blue, slightly protuberant eyes. He laid his papers carefully on his knee, but he did not speak for a moment.

In the odd silence which followed everything in the room appeared to be motionless, so that each face was registered photographically on Calvin's mind. He saw the guards by the door and the strange, barbaric robes of the Prince's retinue, so completely out of place among the rather ugly modern furnishings. He and Captain Hamby were standing in the center of it all, for Mr. Holtz with a placid grunt had eased himself back into his chair again. On his left hand he could see Mr. Moto looking grayish white and shaken, and straight in front of him the Prince sat, his narrow eyes glittering, his lean hands upon his knees. Near him by the table was General Shirov, and farther to the right he could see Major Ahara. The saber cuts on the Major's face were livid and his lips moved soundlessly. When General Shirov spoke even his voice was like that of the Russian whom Calvin had first seen on the train, the facile international voice of the born linguist.

"There are some questions I wish to ask you," he said to Calvin Gates. "I have heard the answers, but I wish to hear them from yourself."

His voice had the impersonal courtesy of a magistrate in court.

"I am questioning you for personal reasons. I am General Shirov, sir, in charge of the Russian Intelligence in China. I wish to ask you about a certain silver cigarette case. It would be helpful if you answered voluntarily, for time is very pressing."

There was another silence, and the General looked at Calvin wearily, and Calvin looked back trying to discover what sort of man it was who was speaking. There was no way to discover, because he was cloaked in a careful, unobtrusive sort of anonymity that revealed no trace of character.

"Go ahead," said Calvin Gates, "I'll answer."

"Thank you," said General Shirov. "Do I understand you are an agent for some government?"

"No," said Calvin Gates.

The General's pale eyebrows lifted slightly.

"Do you intend to convey the idea," he asked, "that you became involved in this matter entirely through accident?"

"Yes," said Calvin Gates. The General's fingers caressed the papers on his knee. His eyes were blue and unblinking.

"A very serious matter to be involved in just by accident, do you not think?" he said.

"Yes," said Calvin Gates.

"Very serious and very peculiar," the General said. "You met a Russian upon the train, between Fusan and Mukden, whose name was Boris, who was acting as courier for a young American lady—will you describe him please?"

The nose, the mouth and the protuberant blue eyes were much the same.

"He looked like you," said Calvin Gates.

The General rustled the papers upon his knee.

"That is right," he said, "the gentleman was my brother. Now you may appreciate my interest. My brother approached the American lady upon the train and offered her a cigarette case. You saw her take it, and that same evening my brother called upon you in your room and asked you to take charge of that cigarette case. This seems extraordinary to me, sir. Did it not seem so to you? Why do you suppose he did such a thing?"

The General's blue eyes were cool and passionless.

"He didn't have time to tell me," Calvin Gates answered. "He was disturbed about something. I gathered that there was some danger connected with that cigarette case."

The General nodded and sighed.

"Yes," he said, "some danger, and I understand from Captain Hamby, who is here beside you now, that my brother was killed in your room. For personal reasons I should like to know who killed him. You say you did not, sir."

"I didn't," said Calvin Gates, and suddenly his mouth felt dry and parched. He was a prisoner undergoing ex-

168

amination at a bar of justice, and he knew that there was no particular reason why he should be believed. "Why should I have wanted to kill him?" he added.

"I do not know," the General said. "I am trying to understand your motives, sir." The General raised his hand from his knee and pointed to Mr. Moto. "Did this man kill him?"

"No," said Calvin, "he did not. He came into the room just a moment afterwards. I think he was surprised." In the silence that followed, Major Ahara drew a deep sibilant breath and stared across the room toward Mr. Moto.

"We will leave that matter for the moment," the Russian said. "After this, you went to the lady's room and she gave you the cigarette case, and you kept it. Why did you do that?"

Calvin Gates hesitated because it was a hard enough question to answer.

"I took it because I thought she would be in danger," he said. "I kept it because I thought we would be in danger anyway, with or without that cigarette case." He looked at Mr. Moto and Mr. Moto stared back at him stonily. "I thought that she and I might be safer if I kept it."

"Yes," General Shirov said. "Were those the only reasons?"

"I guess not," Calvin answered. "I guess I wanted to see what was going to happen. It made me forget some things about myself."

"Oh," said General Shirov, "some things about yourself? And you wished to protect the lady? That is peculiar, sir. When Captain Hamby asked you for this cigarette case you did not give it to him. Why did you not?"

"Because I didn't trust him," Calvin said.

For the first time in that interview the General's wide blue eyes left Calvin's face and turned toward Captain Hamby.

"That is something which I can believe," he said. "Captain Hamby promised us delivery and I find a Japanese here dealing with him."

Captain Hamby's face wrinkled into a hard, bright smile. "The Major came here," he said. "I didn't ask him.

169

I'm always willing to talk business, Shirov. My word, it's coming your way, isn't it?"

"It is coming my way," said General Shirov, "because I have confided in you the latest news from Moscow—that is the only reason. Otherwise I would be the one to be marched outside."

"Righto," said Captain Hamby genially. "We have to use the tools at hand, General. Now if you want to talk business with the Prince—"

"One moment," said General Shirov, "one moment, please. I wish to ask this man another question. I do not trust you, Captain Hamby, about this cigarette case. I have not seen it yet. Now sir, if you please . . . You did not give that silver case to Captain Hamby, you kept it because you wished to protect the lady, and yet you gave it back to her and left her in Peiping. How did that protect her?"

Calvin felt his face redden. Instead of being dignified, he had been foolish, and everything he had said sounded like a tissue of falsehood, although it had only been the truth.

"I quarreled with her," he answered; "but I came up here to find her."

General Shirov's face relaxed into a pale, thin smile.

"That will do I think," he said. "Who is paying you, Captain Hamby or the Japanese?"

Calvin shrugged his shoulders.

"No one's paying me," he answered. "You can believe what I said or not."

"Perhaps," said General Shirov, "when I see the cigarette case—"

Captain Hamby took a step forward and his eyes were bright and angry. The Prince leaned backward in his chair and spoke in his high, thin voice.

"General Shirov," he said, "Captain Hamby has it in his pocket. You shall make your offer. There is only one thing which I must know first. I am sorry that my English is so slow. I was taught by an Englishman. He was brought by my father from Peiping, but that was long ago. It is the only language that everyone can understand, you and the Japanese."

170

"Excellency," the General answered, "your English is very good. What is it that you want to know?"

The Prince looked about him with a serene, cool dignity. "Tonight I am thinking of my people. If I sell to you, Japan will be my enemy. How can I be sure that my people will be protected? That is what I wish to know. Will a strong Russian army move to Ghuru Nor?"

The Russian agent spoke eagerly.

"There can be no doubt of it, Your Excellency," he answered. "I was at the concentration point a week ago. They are only waiting for the message. If Japan begins further pressure on North China, three divisions will move at once into Ghuru Nor."

There was another of those strange silences. Calvin Gates could feel his pulses beating. Out of the corner of his eye he saw Mr. Moto moisten the corner of his lips and heard him sigh.

"Well, you'll never have a better chance," Captain Hamby said. "There's the man right in front of you who is giving the Japanese troops their orders. My word, he's your prisoner just as soon as you pay the money. You've seen the papers in your pocket, haven't you?"

The Russian took the papers from his knee and set them on the table.

"They would appear correct," he said. "But I do not understand how he allowed you to take him. There is something that is not right."

A sudden noise at the right of the room made Calvin turn. Major Ahara had leapt out of his chair before anyone could lay a hand upon him and in a single bound he had reached the center of the room.

"It is true that there is something that is not right," he said. "The man sitting there is a traitor to his country."

Mr. Moto moved uneasily in his chair.

"Please," he said, "please."

"Yes," said Major Ahara, "a traitor to your emperor. You meant that message to be delivered. You allowed yourself to be brought here with the orders on you. Answer me if that is not so. You cannot answer."

"Please," said Mr. Moto, "that will be enough."

"Yes," said Captain Hamby. "My word, it will. Windy

little beggars, you Japanese," and he seized Major Ahara's shoulders.

At the same instant the Major struck at Captain Hamby's arm and the Captain staggered backward with a choking cry of amazement. The room was filled with a confused clamor that sounded like the yelping from a kennel. A dark-gowned man lunged at the Major and missed him. An instant later the Japanese had tripped up the guard by the door and snatched it open. Then he sprang outside with Captain Hamby just behind him. The report of a pistol sounded in the compound, and then a second shot. Mr. Holtz pushed past the crowd at the door. The Prince called out a high, sharp order, but he had not risen from his chair.

At its call the noise in the room died down.

"Hamby," shouted Mr. Holtz, and Captain Hamby's voice answered cheerily from the dark outside:—

"It's all right, Holtz, the beggar's through." And then Captain Hamby sauntered back deliberately through the open door as though he had just stepped out to get a breath of air.

"Smile," Captain Hamby was humming, "smile, smile."

"My friend," said Mr. Holtz, "was that necessary? I told you I wanted none of that in here."

Captain Hamby's face wrinkled in his most exasperating smile.

"Just a peaceful merchant, aren't you, Holtz?" he said. "You're in this the same as everybody else. My word, the beggar was running like a rabbit. We couldn't let him get away."

"But he would not have got away," said Mr. Holtz, and the flesh about his eyes had gathered into dangerous little wrinkles. "Did I not tell you this was to be done out beyond if it was necessary? An officer, a Japanese officer—it is dangerous."

"To hell with the Japanese officers," Captain Hamby said. "You heard what Shirov told us, didn't you? This country will be Russian next week."

"I am not sure," said Mr. Holtz. "We cannot yet be sure."

172

"My word," said Captain Hamby, "you heard Shirov. We've done business with Shirov. We're sure already."

Then in the pause that followed, Mr. Moto spoke, and the contrast of his voice coming so suddenly after Captain Hamby's unmusical speech made every word decisive.

"I am so sorry that you did that," Mr. Moto said. "He was a very good officer. We had differences of political opinion, but he was very nice. I am so very, very sorry."

"Sorry, are you?" Captain Hamby said. "You'd better be sorry for yourself."

Mr. Moto looked at the Prince and at the Russian agent and then at Captain Hamby. His gold fillings glittered in a polite, intelligent smile.

"You mean I shall be liquidated also?" Mr. Moto said.

"Clever little beggar, aren't you?" Captain Hamby said. "You let yourself in for it, didn't you?"

Mr. Moto folded his hands on his lap.

"Perhaps," he said, "and perhaps it is time to make myself clear. You will not liquidate me yet I think. I know so much of Mr. Holtz and so much of you all. I have such a very high opinion of General Shirov. You are all so very, very clever. I know so very well what you are thinking—that, when we are no longer useful, this young American gentleman and I will be eliminated. Do you mind if I explain myself?"

"It don't matter," said Captain Hamby. "We haven't got the time."

"But Mr. Holtz interrupted.

"One little minute," he said. "I want to hear what he says."

"And so do I," said General Shirov. "I want to understand."

"Thank you, General Shirov," said Mr. Moto, "so very, very much. I know you may be puzzled to see me here. My poor compatriot, the Major, was so very, very right. I wished that you would receive the cigarette case with the message it conveyed. I hoped so much that your brother would bring it to you, but there was so much opposition on the part of my own countrymen, so embarrassing to me. I am so afraid that your brother was alarmed when he saw me on the train. I hoped so much that he would bring it safely. I am so sorry for his accident. He was such a clever man."

General Shirov looked at Mr. Moto distrustfully, as though there might be an infernal machine in Mr. Moto's pocket.

"So you wanted me to get that message," he said. "That is kind of you, but the reason is not clear."

Mr. Moto smiled a golden, confidential smile. "Excuse me," he said, "I know so well it sounds irregular. I am so afraid that you might suspect me. If I had not been afraid, I should have been in touch with you myself. You are such a very brilliant man, General Shirov, and we have known each other so long and so unhappily. I was afraid if I came here freely that you would draw away and I wanted so very much to see you face to face. So much simpler for us both. I did not wish you to be alarmed, General Shirov. That is why I arranged for Captain Hamby to capture me. It seemed the only way that we might meet face to face—so very naturally."

The Russian had a peculiar and intent expression. Mr. Moto might have been a page of very fine print that he was trying to read.

"You wished to see me," he said. "Why did you wish to see me?"

Mr. Moto's expression had grown serious.

"Please," he said. "I wish that matters might settle themselves in a happier way, but I am so very much afraid that one of us will not leave this place. We understand such affairs so very, very well. You are here for information and so am I. It is your desire to find out what action my country will take toward China. I could tell you now, but you would not believe. That is why I have arranged for you to receive a message from your own sources. I have arranged it against the advice and wishes of so very many people."

"Yes," said General Shirov, "and what do you desire?"

Mr. Moto sighed.

"My desire is so very, very simple," Mr. Moto said. "There have been so many debates about it. Will Russia intervene if we move farther into China? We have tested the situation at the Amur River, but we are still not

174

sure. If ever your great country will act, it will do so when you receive this message. It will be like a train of powder set alight. You and I know the situation so very, very well. We have our own intelligence in Moscow. If your country will strike, it will do so now, without an ultimatum or a declaration. Such formalities are so very, very silly. The decision must be already made I think. Your army will advance immediately to take up positions at Ghuru Nor. If it does so, we may know that we may expect an intervention. I wish to see if it does so, and I have done more than that."

Mr. Moto paused and rubbed his hands, but Shirov did not answer.

"Yes," said Mr. Moto. "I have done more than that. I have incurred the enmity of many important persons. I am risking my own honor. I have allowed myself to be taken with military secrets in my possession. You have already read the orders on the table? There is not a Japanese unit within two hundred miles of Ghuru Nor. You have your chance this evening—one which will not come again—and I have given you this chance. It is so important to see whether your country takes action that I have seen fit to precipitate the opportunity. This, please, is my own responsibility. I wonder what will happen when you see the message? I will tell you what it will say."

Mr. Moto paused again and glanced about the room. Captain Hamby was frowning and the Prince sat motionless and Mr. Holtz had craned his thick neck forward. The peaceful look had left the Russian's eyes.

"Yes," said Mr. Moto, "I will tell you. The day after tomorrow there will be a series of incidents outside of Peiping which will lead to demands on five Chinese provinces. If your country intervenes, I think it will be now or never." Mr. Moto rubbed his hands together.

"I think we will find out tonight. The Prince will be so interested and so will Mr. Holtz. I know so much of Mr. Holtz."

Mr. Moto turned toward the fat man and smiled.

"Mr. Holtz has worked so hard for Russia, but he has so very many commercial interests that he must consider

175

other matters. He has a wireless with a short-wave sending-set in the next room of this house."

Mr. Holtz gave a startled grunt and Mr. Moto smiled again.

"Do not let it alarm you, please," Mr. Moto said. "Our intelligence is very good. Mr. Holtz will send a message and will get an answer in a very little while, and General Shirov may listen. Mr. Holtz will tell us whether there will be a movement toward Ghuru Nor. He will want so much to know in order to decide what he must do in order to help himself. We shall all be so interested. You will be able to get the answer I think, Mr. Holtz."

"Yes," said Mr. Holtz, "since you know so much. They will send orders here at once if they start to move. It is—arranged."

"I thought so," Mr. Moto answered. "It is so very, very nice. We shall know the news so soon, and the Prince will be so relieved and Mr. Holtz will be so relieved. They will both know which side to take. And then—if definite action is taken I shall be so very happy to kill myself. On the other hand it will be so very different. If there is no move I am so afraid that General Shirov must kill himself. Yes, I think that we shall liquidate the situation. It is my own idea."

Mr. Moto glanced brightly about the room.

"It is so very nice that everything is so well arranged," he said. "Do not look so anxious, Mr. Gates. Personally, I do not think that Russia is going to move. I hope so much for your sake, Mr. Gates. I hope so much I have made myself clear. Thank you so much for allowing me to speak."

Captain Hamby swayed backwards on his heels.

"While you've a lucifer to light your fag," he hummed, and no one interrupted him. "Clever beggar aren't you, Mr. Moto? So darned bright."

"Thank you," said Mr. Moto, "so very, very much."

There was no doubt that Mr. Moto had made himself clear to everyone. Whether the rest of them believed or not, Calvin Gates believed him. He had seen enough and heard enough so that there could be no mistake, and now everything that Mr. Moto had said or done was intelligible. He had accomplished everything which he had set out to do, and now he sat with his hands folded in his lap.

"Perhaps," Mr. Moto said, "Mr. Holtz will open communications upon the wireless. There should be a message soon."

"My word," said Captain Hamby, "this is jolly good. Get the buzzer going, Holtz."

Without answering, Mr. Holtz walked to the far end of the room and opened the door and Calvin Gates had a glimpse of a table covered with electrical apparatus.

"Well," said Mr. Holtz, "everything is ready."

The Russian stood up and there was a note in his voice that had not been there before. Calvin felt the floor unsteady beneath him because he knew what was coming.

"Hamby," said Shirov, "hand me that cigarette case, please. It will tell if this is true."

"One minute." The Prince spoke softly. "What price will you pay me?"

The serious, intent expression left the Russian's face and changed into a thin, cool smile.

"We will discuss that later," he said. "Mr. Moto's presence makes bargaining unnecessary. The corn between the millstones should not ask for money, Excellency. Give me that cigarette case. Give it to me quickly."

"My word," said Captain Hamby, "that's no way to talk."

"You will be paid when this is over," said General Shirov. "The cigarette case please. We must see if this is true first."

"Now," said Captain Hamby, "that's no way to talk. Here it is, look at it for yourself."

He whipped a cigarette case from his inside pocket and handed it to General Shirov. The Russian snatched it out of Hamby's hand and stared hard at the cover. He did not speak immediately, but anyone who watched him could have told that something was wrong.

"My word," said Captain Hamby, "what's the matter?"

"What does this mean?" The Russian's voice was thick. "This is not the case."

"Not the case?" said Mr. Moto, and his face went chalky white.

The Prince was out of his chair. He had turned from a motionless Chinese portrait into a figure of the god of war. He shouted something in his own language and Hamby answered back.

"This is too much," General Shirov shouted.

"Wait a minute," said Captain Hamby, "wait," and he ran to the door.

"I think," said Mr. Moto, "that he has gone to get the young lady, and I do not think she has it. I think it is in this room."

"Where in this room?" Shirov asked.

"Please," said Mr. Moto, "do not excite yourself. I am as anxious as you, believe me." He glanced soberly at Calvin Gates. "I think the young gentleman there has it. So sorry, Mr. Gates."

CHAPTER 21

THE PRINCE STARED hard at Calvin Gates and barked out an order. It was the moment for which Calvin Gates had been waiting, but now that it had come he did not feel wholly adequate to meet it. The men with whom he had to contend were as desperate as he was and, compared with their experience, his was like a child's. He had never seen Mr. Moto so profoundly agitated. The Prince and the Russian agent were both so stirred that they could not conceal their feelings. Surprise, indignation and distrust sounded in their words and swept across their faces.

"It is not him," he heard Mr. Holtz call behind him. "It is that Hamby, he has got it."

One of the Prince's men grasped Calvin's shoulder.

"Take your hands off me," said Calvin Gates, and he felt more sure of himself now that he was speaking. "I haven't got that cigarette case, but I know where it is."

His announcement had a quieting effect and the quiet was reassuring. He stood there in the center of that drama, momentarily master of the situation, and he knew that he must make the most of it. But he paused before he spoke again, careful not to hurry, watching the faces in front of him.

"Ah," said General Shirov, "so you know where it is." The Prince walked forward with a quick stamp of his heavy boots and stopped in front of him—a fantastic figure in his peaked cap, his blue gown and his pigtail.

"You will tell us," the Prince said in his high, slow voice, "at once."

The narrow, dark eyes of the Prince were ugly, but with an effort Calvin Gates grinned back at him.

"Well," he asked, "how much will you give me, Prince?"

"One moment." Mr. Moto spoke quickly. "If I may say a word to Mr. Gates, please. It will do no good to force him I am afraid. He is such a stubborn man, but he will be reasonable when I explain. It is not a time to be difficult, Mr. Gates. You must understand that we are in danger. The Prince is so very angry, and General Shirov is so very angry. It may appear a small matter, but I assure you the cigarette case is vitally important please. Its loss delays everything. Until General Shirov sees it, how can he believe what I have told him? How can the Prince understand his situation? No doubt you think you are gaining something by this delay, but excuse me you are not. If we do not find this article promptly, I am so afraid it will be so very unfortunate for you. I am sure you will be reasonable, Mr. Gates."

There was no mistaking Mr. Moto's deep anxiety.

"I assure you, Mr. Gates," Mr. Moto added, "that there is nothing subtle in what I say."

The whole situation was ironical, but he had learned a good deal from Mr. Moto's subtlety. For once he was able to match his own wits against Mr. Moto's, and to speak in the same polished phrases.

"There is only one trouble," he said. "It is that our points of view are different, Mr. Moto. I do not care about the Russo-Japanese situation. The only thing I care about is personal freedom and my neck."

"Of course," said Mr. Moto gently, "that is so very logical, Mr. Gates, but please, if you are stubborn, you will be made to tell and that will not be very nice. Here is

Miss Dillaway I think. I am so sure that she will agree with me."

The door of the bungalow had opened and Captain Hamby, with a firm grasp on Miss Dillaway's arm, was pushing her into the room.

"There's no use arguing," he was saying. "You don't want to see Gates killed, do you?"

"I don't know what you're talking about," Miss Dillaway said. She looked very small and lonely, but if she was afraid she did not show it. Her answer was brisk and uncompromising. Her head was defiantly erect.

"Now," said Captain Hamby and he gave her a gentle shake, "that's no way to talk."

Although it was not the time or place for like or dislike, Calvin Gates did not like Captain Hamby's manner. Something had broken down the restraint he had put upon himself, and there may have been some unconsidered reason for his action. He may have realized that he was safe for the moment. He was beside them before he knew what he was doing, and before caution or judgment came into play he had his hands on Captain Hamby and Captain Hamby dropped her arm.

"Here," said Captain Hamby, "here." And Captain Hamby stepped backward and put his hand in his pocket.

"I wouldn't try that," said Calvin Gates. "I know where the cigarette case is, Hamby." And Mr. Holtz had stepped down between them before he had finished speaking. He thought that they would seize him, but no one in the room moved.

"You can leave Miss Dillaway alone," Calvin said. "You all want to know where the cigarette case is, don't you? Well, I'll tell you where it is. Miss Dillaway gave Captain Hamby her own cigarette case, and she gave the other one to me, back there in the shed where you locked us up. Do you want to know what I did when I got it? Would that interest you, Mr. Moto? Would you be interested, Mr. Shirov?"

Calvin walked back to the center of the room. Everyone was giving him full attention although he could not tell even then whether his plan was good or bad.

"I looked at the design very carefully. There were some

little birds and grasses. I remember every detail of that design and I can describe it accurately. If you give me a pencil and a paper I can draw it. I wonder if you get my point. Do you understand me, General Shirov?"

The Russian did not answer immediately, but Mr. Moto's mind was quicker.

"Mr. Gates," Mr. Moto said, "you are a very clever man, so very, very clever. You have of course destroyed the cigarette case."

"Exactly," said Calvin Gates. "It's out there in the shed very badly crushed. You won't be able to put it together I'm afraid, but I have it in my mind. Would you like me to draw it for you? I shall do it right away if we come to an agreement. I shall have to take your word and General Shirov's that one of you will see Miss Dillaway, Dr. Gilbreth, and me safely out of here, and that you will promise not to interfere with us further."

The proposal was received in absolute silence, a silence that was broken by a short, ugly laugh from Captain Hamby.

"So that's your idea, is it?" Captain Hamby said. "Going to be an artist are you, Gates? Don't give it a single thought, gentlemen. You let me have Mr. Gates outside for fifteen minutes, and he'll be begging to draw that picture."

"I've thought of that," said Calvin Gates. "There's only one trouble; you'd never be sure whether the picture was right."

General Shirov stroked his pointed chin thoughtfully.

"You are asking a good deal, my dear sir," he said. "How may we be sure that it is right at any rate?"

Calvin Gates shrugged his shoulders. There was no way for them actually to be sure. Ironically enough they had arrived at a question of integrity and character.

"You'll have to take my word," he said, "just as I have to take your word. It may be a risky business, but it's the only way. I have something that you want and you'll have to take my word. You'll have to believe me when I say that I have no interest in deceiving you. Besides, you will be able to see if I am deceiving you soon enough by what I draw. I've only been in this country two weeks. You can

181

do it this way, or try any other with me, but believe me no other way will work."

"You leave it to me," Captain Hamby began; but General Shirov stopped him.

"That will do, sir," he said. "There must be no further mistakes, there is no time for them. This must be arranged without force. Have you a passport, Mr. Gates? If I may see the visas——"

"I have," said Calvin Gates. "I never thought of that."

General Shirov squared his shoulders and there was a different light in his unblinking blue eyes when he turned toward Calvin Gates.

"Your proposition seems the easiest solution, sir," he said. "When you were telling me your history a little while ago I suspected that you had other interests. Now I think that I was wrong. The passport may be a forgery, but I think not. I shall accept your proposition. I am flattered that you are willing to take my word and I am pleased to give it. I am a different type of man from certain others in this room."

"I thought you were," said Calvin Gates. "Will you agree that none of these other people interfere with us?"

"That will be arranged quite easily I think," General Shirov replied. "I am sorry we are so pressed now, Mr. Gates. I shall hope to make your further acquaintance later. If you will step to the table I have a pencil and paper, and may I ask the lady to come with us also, since she has seen that cigarette case too?"

Mr. Moto placed his hand before his lips and drew in his breath.

"You are so very sensible, Mr. Gates," he said. "It is so wise of you to see that Comrade Shirov and I are the only ones who count. Comrade Shirov is such a very nice man. You may rely upon him absolutely and you may rely upon me. You may be quite safe in assuming that none of these other gentlemen will interfere. They would not dare in any case." His bright, quick glance moved to General Shirov and he sighed.

"Yes, he is so very nice, because he is a gentleman. We give our word and we keep our word. I am so very sorry that he and I should be in collision. So very sorry that we have not time to chat together. We would have so very many interesting things to talk about."

General Shirov's lips curled into a thin smile.

"Yes," he said, "we would have a good deal to talk about."

"There's only one more detail," said Calvin Gates.

Mr. Moto looked startled. "What is that?" he asked.

"Dr. Gilbreth's party, they must be brought out safely."

"Oh," said Mr. Moto, and he smiled at the Prince. "So they are having trouble—that is so like His Excellency. They shall be brought out safely."

The Prince spoke suddenly. "Are you saying that I shall receive no recompense?" he asked slowly, and Mr. Moto beamed back at him.

"I am so afraid," he said. "You should have sold while there was an offer. We must arrange terms later now."

The Prince raised his hand from his knee and pointed at Captain Hamby.

"It was that man who advised me," he said.

"So sorry for Captain Hamby," said Mr. Moto gently. "So sorry that he carried affairs so far. I am so afraid that he should not have brought me here."

"If you step this way please, Mr. Gates," said General Shirov, "this way please, madame."

"Do not hesitate, Mr. Gates," Mr. Moto said cordially. "Either Comrade Shirov or I will be in complete control. The Prince and Mr. Holtz and Mr. Hamby will do what one of us tells them. Ha ha, it is so very funny. I am so sorry that Comrade Shirov should be an enemy of my country, and such a dangerous man."

"So sorry for you, Mr. Moto," General Shirov replied. "Here are the pencil and paper, Mr. Gates."

Calvin sat by the table with the pencil in his hand, and Miss Dillaway stood beside him, and General Shirov and Mr. Moto. He could feel the contagion of their interest as he glanced at the paper. He could hear Captain Hamby and Mr. Holtz arguing loudly at the other end of the room.

"You thought you was so smart, what?" Mr. Holtz was saying. "You thought you was so smart to catch that Japanese."

"Well," the Russian said, "we are waiting, Mr. Gates."

Then Miss Dillaway leaned forward and spoke suddenly.

"Give me that paper, Gates," she said. "You don't know how to draw, I do. There were birds in the grass. Tell me how to draw them." She took the pencil in her small brown hand and glanced at him sideways. "He can't do everything, you know," she added.

CHAPTER 22

"THERE WERE five tufts of grass," said Calvin Gates. "The grass was very high, particularly the large tuft in the center." He closed his eyes in order to remember better. "There was one detail about the grass. All the blades were bending to the left as though the wind blew them."

"Like this?" Miss Dillaway asked.

"Five tufts and the grass bending to the left," General Shirov repeated. "That is how it should be. And now the birds? Were they big or little, Mr. Gates?"

"Small birds," said Calvin Gates. "They seemed to have no tails and their beaks were long like woodcock. Three were flying in a little group over by the right. One was on the ground by the left, two were perched in a grass tuft in the center."

"Like this?" said Miss Dillaway.

Calvin Gates studied the drawing carefully and no one spoke.

"No," said Calvin. "The three birds flying were facing toward the right. One was a little ahead of the other two."

General Shirov leaned forward and picked up the paper and examined it for a moment with his lips pressed tight together.

"Mr. Holtz," he said, "is the wireless ready?"

"Yes, all ready," said Mr. Holtz.

"One moment," said Mr. Moto, "one moment please. Everything is correct? I am so very glad. I am so pleased to rely on Mr. Holtz. We must know at once whether action will be taken. How will you find out?"

Mr. Holtz pursed his small lips.

"I shall ask for instructions," he said. "I shall find out. Never fear. General Shirov understands me."

Mr. Moto rubbed his hands together.

"I am so very sure you will," Mr. Moto said. "It is such a pleasure to rely on Mr. Holtz, who is giving us shelter in his house. Mr. Holtz is a man of property, with so many business interests. Mr. Holtz must be on the strong side."

"That is right," said Mr. Holtz. "I shall find for you what they will do up there."

"So very nice," Mr. Moto said. "We shall know when you get your answer. So sorry, General Shirov, that one of us must go. You understand me, I am so very sure. If your army does not march, I am so afraid that no one here will have much use for you. The Prince understands so well. He will become either Russian or Japanese. He will seize either you or me. Does His Highness understand?"

"I understand," the Prince said slowly. "In the meantime I am hospitable to both you gentlemen."

General Shirov made a quick impatient gesture.

"We have had enough talk," he said. "Everyone understands. They are simply waiting for the message."

He turned and walked away with Mr. Holtz toward the communicating door at the far end of the room.

"Smile," Captain Hamby was humming. "Smile, smile, smile." But he was not smiling.

"General Shirov is so sure," said Mr. Moto gently. "It may be well to have someone there to watch. He will be so disappointed if the answer is not what he hopes. So sorry—but he might forget himself."

The Prince nodded his head at Captain Hamby without answering. Captain Hamby followed to the door of the room where the wireless instrument stood.

"My word," said Captain Hamby, "you think of everything, don't you? He won't get away. I'll see to that."

Calvin Gates stood up and peered down the length of the room. The door was half open and he could see Mr.

Holtz's broad back as he bent over the instrument at the table.

"Such an interesting instrument the wireless," Mr. Moto said. "Will you hand me that pencil on the table and another piece of paper, Mr. Gates? Thank you so very much. Ah, they are calling for the station."

The sharp dot and dash of a spark came across the room, petulantly through the silence.

"Yes," said Mr. Moto, "that is the proper call."

Miss Dillaway put her hand on Calvin's arm.

"What are they doing?" she whispered. "What's happening, Gates?"

"We're out of it," he answered, "so what do you care, Dillaway?"

"Don't be so mysterious," Miss Dillaway said. "I can be interested, can't I? It's a lot better than being locked in a shed with Dr. Gilbreth."

"You can be interested if you like," said Calvin Gates. "There's either going to be a war with Russia or there isn't going to be a war, and that old gentleman in blue is a prince who is waiting to see whether he will ally himself to Russia or Japan, and Mr. Moto has precipitated an incident. Then there's a man in the other room named Holtz who owns this place and sends camels over the desert. He is in the other room now, sending a wireless message, and a very high class Russian spy is in there with him. Mr. Moto and the Russian spy don't get on very well. Depending on the answer to the message, your friend, Captain Hamby, and the Prince will take either Mr. Moto or the spy into custody, and that will be the end of one or the other—that's the picture roughly, and you can be interested if you like, but personally I don't care a hang as long as we're out of it."

"You don't?" said Miss Dillaway. "What's gotten into you, Gates? I thought that this was just the sort of thing you liked."

"Maybe I did," said Calvin Gates, "but I'm tired of it now."

"I suppose you're tired of me too," Miss Dillaway said.

"No," said Calvin Gates, "frankly I'm not. You're more interesting, Dillaway."

"I'm glad to hear it," she answered, "because you won't see anything like this again if I have anything to do with it."

"Do you want to have anything to do with it?" Calvin asked her.

"I don't know that I should mind," she said, "if I understand you rightly. You're interesting sometimes, Gates, but you're not going to get me into a party like this again."

"Look here," said Calvin Gates. "You started this. You were given that cigarette case, I wasn't."

She looked up at him and smiled.

"You need a guardian, Gates," she said. "You can't think straight when you argue, but never mind, I like it. You might be worse."

"So might you," said Calvin Gates.

"I suppose you're disorderly around the house," she said.

"Yes," he said, "I am."

"You would be," said Miss Dillaway. "I suppose—"

Mr. Moto's voice brought him back to the present.

"Will you please not talk?" Mr. Moto said. "Although it is very interesting that Mr. Gates is so disorderly. They are sending the message and I am trying to listen please."

CHAPTER 23

THE SHARP SNAP of the wireless was traveling through the room, and Calvin stood there listening with his hand over the girl's beside him. There were a great many things that he wished to tell her that must wait for some other time. He felt a sense of companionship which he had never experienced with anyone else. He was thinking that they would get on well together, and that they knew more of each other than most people. They had gone a long way together. He remembered when he had seen her first on that small boat. They had gone a long way since that night, and now they were standing in a room heavy with the reek of the Prince's unwashed Mongols. It would be something to remember.

Mr. Moto was writing on the paper on his knee.

"That is very nice," he said. "Your picture was correct I think, although it conveyed more than I thought it would. It was a code message. Shirov has advised that everything is clear."

"Do you know their code?" Calvin asked him.

"A little," said Mr. Moto, "enough to read I think. It is sent in a peculiar manner. We have tried to send false messages, but it has been impossible."

Mr. Holtz came slowly into the room mopping his face on a handkerchief.

"We have sent it," he said. "There should be an answer very quickly. We have asked for it. How are you feeling, Mr. Moto?"

Mr. Moto sighed.

"Happy," said Mr. Moto, "very, very happy, Mr. Holtz. I feel that I have done my duty. We shall know the attitude of Russia in such a little while, and that is something, Mr. Holtz. Thank you. I am so obliged for your kind co-operation."

"You are a very cool man, my friend," said Mr. Holtz.

"Thank you," said Mr. Moto, "so very much. It is sometimes so necessary to be cool. There are some things so necessary to die for. It has been so difficult to arrange this evening."

"What's he saying?" Miss Dillaway asked. "Who's going to die?"

"I'll tell you later," said Calvin. "I'm tired of trying to be a hero, Dillaway. I couldn't compete with Mr. Moto even if I wanted."

"Thank you," said Mr. Moto, "so very, very much, but this is simply a business matter. So very sorry that Miss Dillaway should be disturbed by it. We all here know that it is a simple business matter. We have all witnessed similar occurrences, though perhaps not so interesting. Mr. Holtz, have you a cigarette please?"

Mr. Holtz grunted and handed him a box from the table and lighted the match himself.

"Yes, my friend," he said, "you are very cool. I would

not be if I were in your place. Perhaps I am in better touch with Russia."

"Yes," said Mr. Moto "perhaps. You are so very sensible, Mr. Holtz. Thank you very much."

"Holtz," called Captain Hamby, "come back here, Holtz, they're calling."

Mr. Moto flipped the ash from his cigarette. "That is very fast," he said. "I did not think that it would be so fast."

The Prince leaned forward in his chair and looked at Mr. Moto.

"I know so well what you are thinking, my dear Prince," Mr. Moto said. "It must be so very difficult for you. I know what you are thinking. It is not very nice for me, to have that answer come so fast. It indicates that they must have been waiting, and that everything has been arranged. No, it is not very nice. I am so very glad that you have arranged suitably for yourself, Mr. Gates. I am sure that you may rely on General Shirov. I am so sorry that Miss Dillaway should be disturbed."

Mr. Moto wrote a line on the paper on his knee and folded it.

"Mr. Gates," he said, "may I ask a favor please? I am so very afraid that things are going badly. I hope so much that you will leave China promptly. When you are in Tokyo would you call on the gentleman at this address? He is a very distinguished gentleman and he is so very nice. It may be that he will introduce you to an even more distinguished gentleman. Will you simply tell him please that I arranged the matter in spite of difficulty? He will understand so clearly what I mean. Tell him that I have been so happy to have been of service."

Calvin took the paper.

"I don't see what you mean," he said, and Mr. Moto drew in his breath politely.

"I am so afraid that you will see in just a minute," Mr. Moto said. "It is not nice that their reply should come so quickly. I am so afraid that it means that they are grasping the opportunity. The plan was to give every possibility to the Russian command. They have it and I am so afraid that they are taking it. It was what we wished to know, whether or not they would act. I was so afraid that they are acting now."

There was a stir at the far end of the room and Mr. Moto started and turned his head. Calvin saw Captain Hamby standing tense and motionless, staring through the half-open door of the room where the wireless instrument was kept. And then there was the sound of a shot. Captain Hamby shrugged his shoulders and turned upon his heel.

"Smile boys," Captain Hamby was humming. "Smile boys, that's the style. Banzai for Japan!"

Mr. Moto had started up from his chair and Calvin Gates had put his arm around Miss Dillaway's shoulder. The sound of the shot had made him feel sick and weak, but he did not want her to know it. He held her close to him and whispered to her quickly.

"It's going to be all right, Dillaway," he whispered. "Don't let it bother you, Dillaway."

"I'm not," she answered him faintly, "I'm not bothered at all."

Mr. Holtz walked out of his wireless room, mopping his face, and the damp, heavy folds of his cheeks looked pale, like a moon in a cloudy sky.

"Shirov, he has shot himself," he said.

"Yes?" said Mr. Moto sharply, "yes?"

Mr. Holtz pursed his lips and thrust his handkerchief into his trousers' pocket.

"Those Russians," said Mr. Holtz. "I am finished with those Russians. There is always trouble up there, always difficulty. The GPU have arrested Shirov's chief and two generals, and what orders do we get? *There must be no incident to provoke Japan.* They will just stand and do nothing!"

Mr. Moto placed his hand elegantly before his lips.

'So interesting," he said, "so very, very interesting. I must have possession of the message if you please. It will mean so much. So sorry that Comrade Shirov should have been obliged to shoot himself, although it was so necessary. He was such a dangerous man, but he was very nice. He always tried so hard."

Mr. Moto paused and rubbed his hands together briskly.

"Everybody tries so hard, but ideas are so very, very different. I try so hard, and Mr. Holtz, he tries so hard, and so did poor Major Ahara. He tried so hard to have me eliminated several times. So very nice that everything is settled."

Mr. Moto turned about briskly and clasped his hands and bowed to the Prince.

"We shall be so glad to draw an agreement, my dear Prince," he said, "paying you for permission for our troops to assist you in defending your territory. It will be so nice to co-operate with you, my dear Prince."

"I hope," said Mr. Holtz heavily, "that I may have a trade agreement."

Mr. Moto smiled genially at Mr. Holtz.

"Our trade commission will be so glad to co-operate," Mr. Moto said. "You will be so glad to agree to handle only Japanese products, I think. All that Japan wants of anyone, of China or anyone, is economic co-operation and a cordial understanding."

Captain Hamby grinned and his hard gray eyes twinkled.

"My word," said Captain Hamby, "that's all that anyone wants, just a cordial understanding."

Mr. Moto looked at Captain Hamby unsmilingly.

"One moment please," he said. "May I say one word to the Prince in private, just one little word?"

Mr. Moto walked to where the Prince was sitting and whispered in his ear, and the Prince blinked his narrow eyes, and touched the shoulder of the man beside him, and said something in a gentle undertone.

"Well," said Captain Hamby, "what's the secret? My word, we're all friends aren't we?"

"So nice," said Mr. Moto, "that we are all friends."

"Here," cried Captain Hamby, "what's all this?"

The two guards who were standing behind the Prince's chair had moved before he spoke and were pointing their rifles at him. There was a hoarse, monosyllabic order and two more guards leveled their rifles. Captain Hamby's hand moved toward his pocket, but he must have thought better of it, for he finally stood stock-still.

"Not here," said Mr. Moto, "it is disturbing to the lady. Would you be kind enough to lead Captain Hamby outside please. So sorry, Captain Hamby, that you should have killed an officer of the Japanese army. Major Ahara was so very nice. Please do not be alarmed, Miss Dillaway. If you will show the lady a chair, Mr. Gates, do you not think it would be very nice if we had a cup of tea? The Prince will be so glad to join us I think, and Mr. Holtz will be so glad to get it. I am somewhat exhausted, please, but everything is so very nice."

The End